I0571287

CENTERFOLD

KRIS NORRIS

Centerfold
ISBN # 978-1-78430-392-1
©Copyright Kris Norris 2015
Cover Art by Posh Gosh ©Copyright January 2015
Interior text design by Claire Siemaszkiewicz
Totally Bound Publishing

Published in 2015 by Totally Bound Publishing, Newland House, The Point, Weaver Road, Lincoln, LN6 3QN, United Kingdom.

Totally Bound Publishing is a subsidiary of Totally Entwined Group Limited.

CENTERFOLD

Dedication

To Jess and Chris — partners in crime and fellow
procrastinators. I love you ladies.

Chapter One

Glade Manor – home of Spyce Magazine.

"That's it, Scarlet. Now cross your ankles...a bit more... Good. Hold still."

Detective Scarlet Reid tried not to breathe—afraid any movement would bare her breasts even more. The camera already had a full view of her ass as she posed on the fluffy white carpet, chin resting on bent fingers, feet crossed at the ankles. She didn't need her nipples on center stage too. Not that she had much choice. What was supposed to be a two-day assignment with nothing more revealing than swimwear had quickly snowballed into a full-blown nude photo shoot. And unless she was willing to break her cover, her only option was to play along—pretend each click of the camera didn't make her skin crawl.

She looked at her reflection in the mirror behind the photographer. Her brown hair hung in long curls, the red Christmas hat tilted off to one side, and, other than the leather version of elf shoes laced up her feet, she was completely bare. She cringed inwardly. The guys at the station would never let her live this one down.

"Nice, now push your chest out just a bit. We want men dying to see what your nipples look like, so give them just a hint."

The bastard's voice was just a bit too eager, too raspy to be professional. She'd heard the other women talk about him—John Everett. How he had a penchant for touching the girls, whether they gave him permission or not. That he used his position to force himself on them. She sighed. Most of the women she'd met were young, naïve. Girls who had lost their way and were hoping this one magazine spread would be their ticket to fame. And if that came at a price, most seemed willing to chalk it up to the business.

"Pinch them for me, sweetheart. I need them hard."

She hated the endearment, his voice making the word sound tainted. A dizzy feeling swirled through her head as she placed her fingers against her breasts, rolling her nipples until they puckered against her skin, the tips slightly reddened.

"Much better. Now lift up just a bit…"

She resumed her position, arching her back slightly, cringing when Everett hummed his approval. The sound sent a shiver racing down her spine, the unspoken innuendo making her stomach roil. A throaty huff rasped behind the creep, and she chanced a glance at her partner standing off to Everett's left. Roman leaned against the wall, his dark eyes focused on her. He swept his gaze down her body, pausing where her nipples peaked. Heat danced along her skin when he locked his gaze on hers, the intensity in his stare more than unnerving. He'd never looked at her like that before.

"Great work, Scarlet." Everett straightened beside his camera, capping the lens. "If that doesn't make grown men wish for their own Christmas angel, nothing will."

She feigned a smile but knew it didn't reach her eyes. She accepted the robe he handed her. She pushed to her feet, ignoring the way he leered at her before she managed to wrap the soft terry around her, belting it at her waist.

"You're very beautiful, Ms. December. I'm glad Mr. Glade decided to shoot a teaser pose with all of next year's centerfolds. Men will be aching to see your full spread." Everett moved closer, drawing his finger along her arm, a flash of black ink on his wrist as he lingered a bit too long. "Perhaps you'd like to continue this shoot…in private?"

Scarlet stepped back just as Roman grabbed the man by the scruff of the neck and threw him against the wall.

"I thought I'd made it clear. Scarlet's my lover." He inched his face closer, ruffling the creep's collar. "She's not interested in playing with you."

The man laughed. "You know something, Roman? You keep claiming she's yours, but I haven't seen you so much as kiss her outside this room." He pushed Roman back and smoothed the front of his shirt. "I've been watching you two. Sure, you go to all the games, but you don't participate in any of them. Why, just this afternoon there was a pussy-eating contest." Everett licked his lips as he shifted his gaze to her, his focus lingering on her crotch. "I don't recall seeing her sweet little cunt up there on display, your head wedged between her thighs." He turned back to Roman, a sneer spreading across his lips. "I'm starting to think maybe you two aren't what you appear to be.

There're rumors the cops are trying to infiltrate events like this. Maybe—"

"Do I look like a cop?" Scarlet moved in beside Roman. "Please, give me some credit. I learned early that when you've got breasts and an ass like mine, you don't have to do more than wiggle them to make a living." She wrapped her hands around her partner's arm, easing into his embrace. "Roman's just following my lead. I don't mind posing nude, Mr. Everett, but I'm a bit shy when it comes to public displays."

Everett eyed her. "Shy?" He shook his head. "If you say so. But if you don't want me to pass my suspicions along to Mr. Glade, you're going to have to convince me."

Roman's cock peaked against her at the man's words, and she couldn't halt a soft whimper from feathering across his shoulder. He bent down, brushing his lips along her neck, tasting the sweet spot behind her ear.

He arched an eyebrow at Everett. "What exactly did you have in mind?"

"There's no one else here and this was my last shoot." Everett waved at the bearskin rug. "If you want me to believe you're her lover, then show me." He patted his chest pocket. "I'll even take you with me tonight to meet my supplier. I know you both want more of what's been floating around."

Scarlet stilled. This was it. Their big break. Seven days on the damn job, and they were literally one fuck away from nailing this drug dealer and his mob supplier. But could she go through with it? Would Roman? She clenched her jaw, not sure how to answer, when Roman's voice sounded above her.

"So you want to watch?" He shrugged. "That's cool. I'm sure Scarlet won't mind one set of eyes watching her. But you'd better be serious about your meeting. That shit you've been trying to pass off as cocaine isn't going to cut it." He slid his hand down and cupped the curve of her ass. "My baby deserves the best."

Everett mumbled something back, but it got lost in the thrumming of her heart. Roman was going to do it — make love to her, right there on the damned floor of the studio. While another man watched! The world dipped a moment before she realized she was in Roman's arms, moving over to the rug.

She looked up at him, captivated by the erotic gleam in his eyes. He didn't look upset... He looked like a hunter claiming his prize after a long, hard chase. And if his cock was any indication of his enthusiasm, she had a feeling he was in the mood to put on quite a show.

"Roman..."

"Easy, darling." He lowered her to the rug, tucking a stray lock of hair behind her ear. "I know this wasn't how you envisioned me loving you tonight," he began, his voice loud enough for Everett to hear. "But under the circumstances..." He motioned back to where the man had taken root in a chair. "Just close your eyes and feel everything I can do for you."

She tried to speak, but he caught her lips in a primal kiss, dipping his tongue into her mouth like a man who'd dreamed the act a thousand times. He traced every hollow, every dip and curve, until his taste was all she knew. She moved with him when his fingers twirled through her hair, tilting her head to deepen the kiss. His soft moan drew her back, his lips still touching hers, their breath mixing.

"I'd like to say I'm sorry, but I've wanted you for a long time, and I don't plan on wasting any opportunity I'm given." He kept his voice low, the sound barely reaching her, as he kissed the soft shell of her ear, making her arch into him. "By the time I'm finished, no one in the room will doubt you're mine."

Scarlet moaned as he slanted his lips over hers again, this kiss more demanding than the last. He didn't taste her this time, he conquered, thrusting inside, devouring her mouth, eating her without mercy, without hesitation. Every flick of his tongue sent a pulse to her groin, heating her juices until they coated her pussy. Hell, if he didn't stop soon, she just might come.

Roman pulled back, swiping his tongue along her lower lip. "Damn, you're beautiful—your lips all full and wet." He drew a deep breath. "Smells like your other lips are the same." He bent forward, placing a quick kiss on her nose. "Now, let me see your sexy body."

Scarlet snagged her lip as he pulled the edges of her robe apart, easing it over her shoulders until it pooled around her wrists. She skirted a look at Everett. He sat in the chair, brushing his cock through his jeans, his gaze focused on her breasts as Roman reached down and held one heavy mound in his hand.

"God, I love your breasts." He grazed his thumb over her hard nipple. "So big and firm. And your nipples... They're so quick to respond." He looked into her eyes. "You like it when I pinch them just a bit hard, don't you?"

She cried out as he tweaked one turgid bud, rolling it around then pulling it firmly away from her body. She couldn't stop from arching into him, begging him to use his mouth. Roman smiled—his reply a heated breath across her skin.

"Oh, yeah. I'm going to use my mouth." He nodded toward her hands. "Now get rid of that robe and hold your breasts for me."

A shiver tingled along her spine. His voice was rough, dominant and edged with a tone she hadn't heard before. Her nipples tightened further as she slipped the fabric off her wrists and placed her hands beneath her breasts, lifting them toward his face.

"Very nice."

Shit, his praise shouldn't make her body cream and her pulse race. She considered herself obnoxiously independent, her career choice a clear indication that she didn't have issues speaking her mind or going after what she wanted. But just hearing that gravely tone wash over her fluttered her stomach until she knew she'd do anything just to have him praise her again.

He leaned in, licking each one. "Like sweet, little strawberries."

He dipped his head down farther, this time taking her full nipple into his mouth. A moan vibrated through her chest as he drew on the hard bud, nipping at it then rolling it around his tongue. She reached for his head, needing to thread her fingers through his thick hair. Roman hummed, plucking her other nipple with his fingers.

"It's too bad you can't have a taste, darling." He repeated the caress, switching sides. "They're absolutely delicious."

Scarlet tilted her head, brushing her hair against the curve of her ass as the hat teetered and slipped to the rug. She thought about tossing it aside, but that meant releasing Roman's head, and she couldn't seem to get her fingers to let go. He pulled back, lifting just enough to meet her gaze.

"Lay back. I can smell your arousal and if I don't get a taste of you soon, I might just die of thirst."

She moved with him, his hand braced against her chest, the other cradling her head. He fanned her hair across the rug as she settled onto the soft fur, still gripping his head.

"Roman." She forced herself to swallow, hoping to ease the dry rasp of her voice. "I'm a bit self-conscious of…"

"Of what?" He circled one nipple with a single finger before looking behind him, smiling at the man now openly caressing his shaft. "Everett?" He flicked it off as if the man was nothing more than a fly as he returned his attention to her. "He's just jealous I'm the one who gets to touch you. Hell, this is as close as he'll ever get to having such a fine piece of ass." He reached down and cupped one pearly cheek in his hand. "And you do have an incredible ass. One I'd love to play with. But first…"

Roman trailed his finger up, drawing it through her narrow slit. He murmured his approval as he brought his drenched finger to his mouth, licking the moisture clean. "Like peaches and cream." He made another pass, dipping deeper. "God, I can't wait until you come all over my tongue." He narrowed his eyes as he gazed at her bare sex. "Okay. Now I want you to open up nice and wide for me. I want our friend over there to see just what he's missing. Every drop of your juice. Every pulse of your clit. I want him to know what a lucky man I am." He hooked his thumbs along the inside of her knees and drew them apart. "Keep them like that, or I'll be forced to punish you. And I'm sure that man would love nothing more than to see your pretty ass spanked."

Scarlet could only nod, shifting her gaze between Roman and Everett. The man was pumping his cock, making it weep with anticipation. Roman brushed her skin, and she skirted her eyes back to him. He eased away, giving Everett a better view of her pussy as he drew her inner lips apart and gazed at her clit.

"So delicate. God, it amazes me how something so fragile brings you so much pleasure." He swirled his finger around the tiny nub, drawing her hips forward. "You like it when I touch you there, don't you? But I think you like it even more when I lick you."

The breath she'd been holding hissed free as Roman dipped his tongue into her sex, before curling it around her clit. Darkness threatened, her body so sensitized she had to will her release away. Too much. Too many sensations, and she couldn't seem to stop the ascent.

"Fuck, Scarlet. I've only just started eating you and already I can tell you're close. Damn, you're such a responsive little minx." He lapped at her. "That's it. Fight it. Wrap your fingers around my hair and make me work for my sweet prize."

Scarlet moaned, and when Roman growled in reply, she couldn't stop another moan from rumbling free. God, he was good. Plunging his tongue deep inside her, then spreading the warm liquid around her clit. She lost track of time, of the man groaning in the background, as Roman slipped his finger inside, touching her deeper than any man ever had.

"Damn, you're tight." He wedged two inside her this time, pushing against her tender flesh. "I'm not going to last long once I get inside you. I've never felt such sweet pressure."

"Oh, God. Please. Please let me come."

She didn't care how desperate she sounded. He'd taken her higher than she'd ever been, and she knew if he didn't let her come soon, she might just melt into a puddle of lust.

Roman chuckled against her flesh, pulsing her clit. "Okay. I'll let you come. Now throw your head back and scream for me."

His name vibrated off the walls, as his mouth latched around her clit, his fingers pumping her slick flesh. Everett groaned his release as hers rocked through her, sending her pussy into spasms, her vision exploding into shards of colored light. Roman hummed against her flesh, the sound of him lapping up her juice only prolonging her orgasm. She'd never come that hard before and was somewhat frightened at the thought of him making love to her. What if she lost consciousness? Or worse. What if she lost her heart?

Scarlet fluttered open her eyelids just as Roman moved over her, his cock nudging her weeping sex. She didn't know when he'd stripped off his clothes, but the feel of his hot flesh against hers made another ripple of pleasure shiver through her. He smiled at her reaction, inching inside her, when Everett's voice sounded behind them.

"Fuck this. I can't see anything if you fuck her that way." The man scraped his chair closer, remnants of his climax still clinging to his skin. "I want her on her hands and knees. I want to see those tits bounce as you pound her from behind. What good is having an ass like that if you don't use it?"

A deep flush laced heat down her neck as the man moved into a more favorable position. She'd always considered her ass to be a bit on the ample side, its mounds matching the large swell of her breasts. But the way the men at the Manor had been sizing it up, she was starting to see it in a different light.

Roman tensed above her, and for the first time since he'd touched her, she saw uncertainty. She met his gaze, reading his thoughts in the shift of his eyes. He didn't want to take her like that...didn't want to cheapen what they were sharing for the first time.

She smiled and brought her lips to his ear. "Nothing can change what this means to me. So take me anyway you want." She dipped her tongue inside the shell. "You can make it up to me next time. And I'm counting on there being a next time."

Roman grunted, whether from her actions or words, she didn't know. But before she could feel the loss of his cock, he had her flipped onto her knees, one hand wrapped around her hair, the other gripping her waist.

He tugged on the strands, arching her head back as he whispered against her neck. "You'll pay for allowing me to take you like this, and I can't wait to spank that pretty ass. But for now, give him a good show, 'cause he's right. Every man dreams of thrusting against an ass like this."

Scarlet cried out when he connected his hand smartly with her buttocks as he plunged his cock home, sheathing himself inside her. He tugged on her hair again, adding a sharp sting as he pulled his shaft back through her tissues, rimming the edge of her sex with the crown before reclaiming the lost inches, making the muscles on her ass shimmy from the impact.

"Ah, fuck. You're so damn beautiful." He moaned as he slammed home again, locking his sac against her clit. "I'm not going to last long. You're just too damn sexy."

Kris Norris

"Then fuck me, hard!"

She tossed her head back as he tugged more firmly on her hair. God, when had she turned into a masochist? She'd never allowed any lover to inflict even a hint of pain. But every sting of her scalp, every firm slap on her ass only increased her desire until she begged for more.

Roman answered her plea, peppering her cheeks with forceful taps as he drove into her, pumping his hips like a man on a mission. He rode her hard, plunging deep with every stroke until she wondered if she might split. She'd never had a man claim her so completely, taking her to the threshold between pleasure and pain. Every thrust set her on fire, every slap intensifying it until she didn't know which pleased her more.

"Fuck, darling. I can't hold it off. Come for me. Give me what I want."

He released her hip as he smoothed his hand down her thigh, cupping her mound. He paused as he circled his fingers around her sex, touching her skin where it opened to accommodate his driving shaft. He grunted again, sliding his finger up to her clit, rubbing the roughened pad across the tight nub. Her breath hitched as the extra stimulation rocked her higher, suspending her on the verge of climax.

He left her there, hanging, for three agonizing heartbeats before slamming into her. His body clenched, and he tightened his hand around her hair a moment before he shouted her name, the hard pulse of his cock sending her over the edge. She echoed his scream as her pussy milked his shaft until she wasn't sure how he stood the pressure. He tugged her head back, granting him access to the sleek line of her shoulder. Scarlet tried to breathe, to gather any form of control, when his teeth locked around her flesh and her world exploded.

Pain and pleasure merged into one, draining her strength, Roman's grip the only force holding her up. She fell back to earth, her body spent, tears burning behind her closed lids, his name a whisper from her lips. Roman curled into her, easing her against his chest, holding her possessively around the waist. He mumbled something, but all she could do was breathe.

The chair scraped against the floor, the sudden sound startling her. She forced open her eyelids, tensing when Everett stared at her, a cruel smile curving his lips. He stood, yanking up his pants before shuffling over to them, the stench of his aftershave smothering her.

"Now that's how you fuck a bitch." Everett gazed openly at her as he joined them on the rug. "I can see why you want to keep her undercover. She's one hell of a feisty little fuck. Okay, you've proven your claim. Meet me back here...ten o'clock sharp, and I'll take you along. But make sure you bring cash. My supplier doesn't take credit."

Everett's laughter followed him out of the door, the solid thud shattering the intimate atmosphere. Roman sighed against her back, resting his forehead against her head. Uncertainty bunched her muscles as he gave her a squeeze, gently shifting her forward as he eased free of her body. A thousand thoughts raced through her mind, but all she could focus on was the empty feeling between her legs and how cold she felt without him wrapped around her.

His footsteps sounded on the floor behind her, and she took several deep breaths before finding the courage to turn, inhaling sharply as she watched him tug his briefs over his hips. God, the man had a perfect ass, the muscles rippling as he adjusted himself before grabbing his jeans and tugging them on. He turned, his gaze traveling the length of her body as she kneeled on the rug, too shocked to do more than stare at him.

He gave her a stunning smile, bending down to offer her the robe. "You okay?"

His words snapped her back to into focus and she nodded, knowing her voice would carry the desperation strumming through her veins. She didn't want to get dressed. She wanted Roman to make love to her again. Gently this time. Have him claim her in another way—one that would ease the erratic pounding of her heart and settle the need clawing at her conscience.

"That's my girl." He darted to the door, checking the hallway before glancing back at her. "All clear. But we really should go...call the lieutenant and arrange for backup. Whoever Everett's supplier is, I don't want to go in there with just our service weapons as cover. Chances are we'll be facing some pretty impressive firepower. We need..."

As his voice trailed off, that wicked mouth of his pursed into a slight frown. She managed to gain her feet, her fingers white-knuckled around the fabric as she held the robe closed, a strange ringing in her head.

"Scarlet."

She gave herself a mental shake, meeting his gaze.

He moved over to her, giving her a tilt of his head. "You sure you're okay?"

She faked a smile, a mixture of terror and desire still flooding her system. Shit. One taste and she couldn't picture loving another man. Couldn't think about her future without him in it. Hell, he'd been her partner for years, yet she'd given more of herself in that one act than in all the time they'd spent together before. She'd surrendered her soul to him and she wasn't sure she could get it back.

She drew herself up. "Fine."

He snorted. "Did you hear a word I said?"

"Sure. The lieutenant…backup. More weapons…"

He sighed, brushing his thumb across her jaw as he leaned in, dropping a light kiss on the corner of her mouth. "I know you probably have a thousand questions, but… Let's just get through tonight. Put Everett's ass in jail and bust whoever's selling him that poison. Once we've wrapped this up, we'll talk. Promise."

She swallowed past the thick feeling in her throat. She recognized the tone of his voice, that look on his face. The way his pitch rose at the end as his lips twitched ever so slightly. He was buying time. Telling her what he thought she needed to hear so they could do their job. God, had it only been his job?

Hurt dropped her stomach and she cursed the tears that threatened to slip free. "I'm fine, Roman."

She moved past him, methodically planting each step, afraid any distraction would send her to her knees. What the hell had she been thinking? Did she honestly think she could just have sex with Roman and not have it mean so much more? Have it mean everything?

Roman huffed behind her as she left the studio, the warm blast of late summer air drying the tears pooling in her eyes. It'd all be over tonight—she just didn't know if they'd finish more than the assignment.

Chapter Two

"You ready?"

Detective Roman Kincaid glanced at Scarlet, frowning when she didn't reply. She stared out of the window of their sedan as they sat in the abandoned parking lot. They'd followed Everett to a warehouse by the pier, waiting for the man to signal them to enter—aware this was the moment they'd been working toward since arriving at the playmate mansion. But the prospect of ending the case didn't hold the appeal it had a week ago. And the reason was sitting next to him.

Roman studied her face in the ghosted reflection of the glass, noting the firm press of her lips and the troubled look in her eyes. She hadn't been the same since they'd left the studio and prepared for the drop.

He groaned inwardly. He'd fucked up. Literally. And he doubted there'd be any turning back—not now that he'd finally gotten a taste of her. Felt her body give beneath him, warm and welcoming as he'd shouted out his release. Hell, he'd half convinced himself that he wasn't really attracted to women. That his feelings for her were a by-product of the long hours together. Her easy acceptance and unparalleled faith in him. But there was no mistaking Scarlet lit him on fire. Made his stomach flutter and his brain go fuzzy. He'd only ever felt that way with one other person.

Warning bells sounded in his head. Despite his doubts, he'd been attracted to Scarlet instantly — from the moment the lieutenant had first introduced her and suggested they'd make a good team. They'd been partners ever since, spending more time with each other than most couples. But he'd managed to keep his growing feelings for her tightly tucked away — until Everett had threatened to expose them and offered him a way out.

And he'd taken it. Taken her — with a force that had surprised him. He wasn't generally that dominant in bed, at least not the first time with a partner. And knowing he'd shown her a side of himself few people were privy to rocked him to the core.

He speared his fingers through his hair, using the slight scrape of his nails to calm himself. He wasn't sure what unsettled him more — that she knew the kind of lover he was or that she'd embraced his firm touch. Encouraged it. He knew she wasn't the type of woman to give up control, and the fact she'd surrendered so completely to him blew his mind.

He cursed under his breath, nudging her with his elbow. "Hey. You with me?"

She frowned, glancing at where his arm still touched her as she exhaled a harsh breath. "I'm a foot away from you. Of course, I'm with you."

"That's not what I meant and you know it."

A strange emotion shaped her features before she punched him in the shoulder. "I'm fine. Just a bit edgy, which is normal, considering we're about to walk into a warehouse full of people who'd love nothing more than to kill us."

"You don't have to do this if it doesn't feel right. Despite what headquarters thinks, this isn't worth dying over."

"Now who's not listening? I said I'm fine. I'll have your back, just as I always do. Nothing's changed."

Roman stilled as her voice cracked slightly on those last two words.

Nothing's changed.

Fuck. He should have talked to her, first, instead of worrying about the case. Even if it'd only been to reassure her that their tryst hadn't been based solely on the situation. That he'd been falling in love with her a bit more every day since they'd first met.

He turned toward her when Everett walked out of the warehouse, the man's body backlit by a harsh light from within the building. Roman pushed aside his other thoughts. He could make it up to Scarlet later, once they'd dealt with the scum inside the building.

"Showtime, darling. Stay close and don't do anything heroic." He snagged her arm as she moved to open her door. "And we *will* discuss everything once this is over. So don't get any bright ideas about ditching me once the cavalry rides in."

Scarlet merely huffed, stepping out of the car as Everett stopped several feet back, that creepy gaze of his roaming her body. Roman clenched his jaw. He should have beaten the fucker senseless instead of allowing him to see even a glimpse of her. Of course, they wouldn't be moments away from breaking their case wide open if he had.

He reached into the backseat, grabbing a briefcase off the floor before climbing out of the car and shutting the door. They'd done what was necessary to get the job done. He'd fix this situation with Scarlet soon. Until then, he needed to focus on keeping them both safe.

Scarlet walked around the hood of the sedan, maintaining a noticeable distance back from Everett as the man waved at them, spinning on his heels and heading toward the warehouse. Roman fell into step beside his partner, unease prickling the back of his neck. He didn't like going into the building blind. But questioning Everett hadn't been an option. The man was already suspicious and despite the lengths they'd gone to mollify those suspicions, Roman knew the creep still didn't fully trust them.

Everett stopped, waiting for them to move in behind him. "Here's how it's going to be. We walk in there. You two stand still while my friend ensures you're clean, then we talk business. You got the money?"

Roman raised the case. "What did you think was inside this? A change of clothes?"

"A mouth like that might just get you a few extra holes." Everett leered at Scarlet. "Of course, I'd be real nice to your girl. Make sure she didn't feel alone."

"Touch her, and you'll be the one who doesn't leave here alive."

Scarlet glanced at him, raising an eyebrow as she gave him a curt shake of her head.

He simply smiled at her. He didn't care if it he stepped over a line. Fuck the line. Keeping her safe was his primary goal, and he wanted Everett to know he meant what'd he'd said. Scarlet was his. Period.

Everett glared at him. "Just do what you're told, and we'll all walk out of here in one piece."

The man motioned them inside. Roman gave Scarlet one last glance then headed into the building. The door closed behind them, glaring light gleaming off the metallic walls. A black suburban sat off to one side, four men flanking the vehicle.

Roman scanned the surroundings as they made their way across the cement pad, noting two more men positioned on an upper level, rifles aimed their way. He watched as a blonde in a skimpy outfit bounced over to Everett then hung off his arm as Everett followed behind them, the man's gaze clearly focused on Scarlet's ass, despite the glare his date gave him.

She nudged Roman, not turning to face him. "Everett is the least of our worries. Those bastards up high have Remingtons. Betting those boys by the suburban have forty-fives."

"Just stick beside me. I'll make sure you get clear when our team busts down the door."

"I don't need you to protect me. I can take care of myself."

"I'm intimately aware of what you're capable of. That doesn't mean I'm going to stand there and watch you risk your life." Roman leaned toward her, still keeping his voice low so only she heard him. "Stick to my ass, or I'll spank yours red."

Her breath hitched for a moment, a muted hum barely reaching him as they stopped in front of the truck. Two men darted forward, patting down their clothes before shaking their heads and returning to their positions. The rear passenger door creaked open, and a tall man in a gray suit stepped out, moving slowly toward them. He looked about forty, with salt and pepper hair and a slim build. He paused beside the other men, visibly measuring them up.

Everett darted forward, a smug smile curving his lips. "Here they are. Just like I promised."

The older man sneered at Everett, stepping slightly ahead of the group. "Your loyalty is the only reason you're still alive. Don't get smug because you did what I pay you to do."

The smile faded from Everett's mouth as he moved back, yanking the woman harder against him. He muttered something under his breath as he stood there, pouting.

Roman eyed the exchange, an uneasy feeling gnawing at him. Something felt off. He inched closer to Scarlet, noting the way she'd tensed. She obviously sensed the same odd vibe he'd picked up on. Pride warmed his chest. Damn, she was good at her job. And if it weren't for the fact the thought of losing her scared the hell out of him, he'd be able to relax a bit — knowing she had his back. But just picturing her injured...

He shoved away the images. Nothing was going to happen to her. Period. He firmed his stance as the older man finally walked up to them, nodding at the briefcase.

The guy gave him a disturbing grin. "Everett tells me you're...unhappy with the grade of cocaine I've been giving him. That true?"

Roman tilted his head, keeping his expression fixed. "We both know you've been cutting it with more than a few fillers. That might fool the average junkie, Mr..."

"Smith."

"Smith?" Roman nodded. "Fine." He raised one hand, drawing it affectionately through the ends of Scarlet's hair. "My girl deserves better. She *needs* better, if you know what I mean. Everett seems to think you can give me what I want. Can you or is this just a waste of my time?"

Smith glared at him. "You're pretty cocky for a playboy model's agent, Mr. Kincaid."

Roman grinned. At least his name hadn't sent off any alarms with Smith. "Have you seen her? She's exquisite. Trust me. Scarlet's the next Marilyn Monroe. Classy, sexy, with curves men would kill for. I'm already getting requests for her to attend a number of political conventions—the kind that don't get publicized. But sometimes she needs a little something extra to keep her going. Either you have that or you don't. Which is it?"

"Oh, I've got it. But what makes you think I'll deal with you?"

"Because you're a businessman and after we shove all the bullshit aside, your sole motivation is money." He laid the briefcase on the hood, punching in the codes to release the locks. He paused, ensuring Scarlet had a chance to see which number he'd inputted, silently informing her he'd released the hidden compartment, as well, before opening the lid. He spun the unit around, exposing the layers of bound bills. "And I have plenty of that."

Smith stared at the case, reaching for it when Roman snapped it shut, pushing it back to Scarlet.

He tsked the dealer. "Not until I know what I'm paying for. And it'd better be a far sight better than what I've seen so far."

Smith glared at him, visually measuring him up before waving his hand. One of the men behind him reached into the truck, removing a small duffle bag. He joined them at the front of the vehicle, handing the bag to Smith.

Smith smiled as he placed it beside the briefcase, slipping the zipper open. "Go ahead."

Roman inched closer, examining the powered contents wrapped in plastic. He held out his hand, waiting until Smith reluctantly gave him a small knife. Roman shook his head, cutting a small slice in the top container, gathering a bit of the contents on the tip of the blade. He pressed his finger into the powder, licking a fraction of it off his skin.

He arched an eyebrow. "Better. But if this is as good as you've got..."

Smith pushed forward, crowding against Roman's chest. "Are you saying my stuff isn't good enough for you?"

"Are you telling me this is really what I came to buy?"

The man hovered within inches of Roman's face before cracking a smile. He punched Roman on the shoulder, shouting out an order for someone to bring him the other bag. Another of Smith's men appeared beside the man, a black bag in tow.

Smith motioned to the hood and the guy lowered the bag, taking the other duffle with him. Roman glanced at the offering, repeating his actions with the new supply. He glanced at Scarlet, giving her a guarded nod. This was what they'd been waiting for.

He turned to Smith. "Now we're communicating. How much?"

"For all of it? One-twenty-five."

"For four kilos? That's a bit steep."

Smith shrugged. "You won't find shit that pure anywhere else. You said you wanted the best. That comes at a price."

Roman made a point of turning to Scarlet, bending low as if discussing it with her. "Lay down cover fire then get your ass to the other side of the truck. Understood?"

Her expression clearly told him to fuck off, that this wasn't her first rodeo, but she nodded, plastering on that fake smile she'd been using since they'd made love.

You mean since you fucked her and walked off without anything more than some token words.

He grunted, silencing the voice in his head as he twisted to face Smith. "Fine. How often can you get this amount?"

"How often do you want it?"

"Monthly."

Smith snorted. "Four kilos a month for her?"

"I didn't say it was only for Scarlet. Just that she deserved the best. My other clients are high-scale. They'll pay to get this grade." He extended his hand. "Do we have ourselves an understanding, Mr. Smith?"

Smith stared at Roman's hand for several moments then shook it, nodding at the bag. "The money."

"Of course. Scarlet."

She moved in close, keeping the case snugged to her chest before giving Smith a devastating smile. Then she shoved the unit forward, hands skimming over the back before the briefcase toppled off the hood, crashing to the floor — the loud noise sparking a chain reaction.

The doors behind them exploded inward, sending shredded bits of metal shooting into the air as plumes of smoke filled the room. Men in uniform swarmed through the gaping hole, bursts of gunfire popping to life.

Scarlet tossed him one of the guns from the briefcase, clipping two of the thugs while he took out the other. Smith scrambled for cover, yelling at Everett to fucking shoot. The man shielded himself with the blonde, yanking her by her hair as he fired toward them. Roman grabbed Scarlet, dragging her behind the truck as a bullet ricocheted off the hood. It grazed his arm, flaring pain up through his shoulder.

"Shit!" Her face hovered in front of his, tears glistening in her eyes. "Roman—"

"It's nothing. Stay down. I'll..."

His words hissed into a gasp as Scarlet's eyes widened. She fisted his shirt, shoving him sideways as she fired, aiming behind him. She got off three rounds before her body jerked twice, knocking her back. She hit hard, head lolling off to one side.

"Fuck, Scarlet!"

He dashed to her side after clearing the immediate area, ignoring Everett's body splayed out on the cement behind him. She'd taken out the bastard, but at what cost?

He kneeled beside her, stomach dropping as blood blossomed on her shoulder, the red color mocking him. "No, no, no."

He clamped his hands against the wounds, cursing when she cried out, her chest heaving beneath him. Shit, it should have been him. She'd yanked him aside and taken the bullets meant for him.

"Easy, darling. Just stay with me."

"Roman."

"Save your strength." He glanced around, trying to pinpoint paramedics amidst the chaos. "Medic! I need a fucking medic!"

"No, Roman." Her eyes rolled back for a moment, her breath stalling.

"God, Scarlet, please. Just lie still and stay with me."

"Youneedtoknow," she mumbled, threading all the words together.

Did she say her feet were cold?

"Hush. Don't talk. Medics are on their way. Just stay with me. Let me see those beautiful eyes of yours."

She offered him a weak smile, eyelids drifting shut.

"Scarlet! Where the hell are the medics?"

He cursed again, scooping her into his arms, holding her tight against him as he ran through the warehouse. Fuckers had probably kept the paramedics outside until they'd secured the scene. He dashed through the doors, looking for a damn ambulance. He spotted one just inside the police line and headed for it.

"Roman."

He looked down as her head lolled against his shoulder. Her blood soaked his shirt, like warm sticky patches of honey on his skin, as her eyelids fluttered then closed. Her lips moved, but no words came out as he laid her down across the stretcher, watching the paramedics swarm over her. He stayed close, his chest too tight to speak, her hand sandwiched between his. She opened her eyes one more time as they lifted her up.

"I love you."

He let her hand slip from his, unable to move as they pushed her into the back. He managed to take a step forward, but one of the medics blocked his way, mumbling something about meeting them at the hospital. He nodded, knowing he should say something in return, but he couldn't think. Couldn't breathe past the lump in his chest as reality slammed back.

Her soft words played in his head as the ambulance hummed to life, sirens wailing, lights casting multicolored dots across the asphalt before it sped off. He stared after it, unable to move when a hand landed on his shoulder. He turned, looking into a pair of blue eyes, the familiar gleam in them threatening to drop him to his knees.

He forced himself to swallow. "Aiden, what—"

"Joint task force, remember? I got the S.W.A.T. guys to let me tag along. Did you really think I'd simply stand by and hope you made it through this meeting alive? What kind of federal agent would that make me? What kind of man?" Aiden offered him an apologetic smile. "Come on. I'll take you to the hospital. You need your arm stitched."

"I'm fine. Scarlet..."

He couldn't say it. Couldn't acknowledge aloud that he might lose her. Fuck, he should have insisted he ride in the ambulance with her. Hold her hand. Talk to her. Instead, she'd blown him away with three small words.

How long had he wanted to hear her say that? To return feelings he wasn't brave enough to show? Yet, the admission only increased the fear tight in his chest, making the simple act of breathing next to impossible.

"I know. But you're in no condition to drive. Please, Roman. Let me take you."

Aiden remained strangely quiet throughout the drive, pulling into parking lot then opening the door for him. He followed Roman inside as Roman headed for the nurse's station, stumbling against it when his balance shifted. The woman behind the desk scowled at him before her gaze landed on his arm. She gave him a knowing smile, motioning to someone behind him.

Roman opened his mouth, when Aiden palmed his back, leading him into an adjoining room. He pointed to the bed, helping Roman up before crowding in front of him. The man's hands rose to his shirt as he began flipping open the buttons, each one making his heart race faster.

Roman snagged Aiden's arm, keeping him from freeing the last button. "Aiden."

The man smiled. "Please. Give me some credit. I'm just helping. Promise. I know now's not the time to cloud your thoughts with anything else. Not with Scarlet's life on the line. But in case you haven't noticed, you're bleeding...rather profusely. Doctor needs to stitch that, buddy, or you'll pass out on us."

Roman sighed, glancing at his arm. Shit. He hadn't even realized he'd been hit that badly—not with Scarlet's blood soaked through to his skin. He nodded, going through the motions, barely noticing the entire procedure. Everything seemed shaded in gray as he finally made his way to the waiting room, staring at the swinging door in the distance, wondering if the next person to walk through it would save his life or end it.

Time bled together until a coffee cup appeared in front of him. A hint of a smile tugged at his lips as he took the offering, shuffling over slightly as Aiden sank into the cushion beside him. The man leaned back, the heat from his body curling around Roman, caressing his skin like a physical touch. He finally built the nerve to look at the guy, regretting the decision as soon as their gazes met. Compassion colored Aiden's eyes, an easy smile tilting his lips.

He nudged Roman with his knee. "I'm assuming the fact you look like a zombie means you haven't heard anything, yet?"

Roman shrugged, wincing as pain shot up his arm before nodding at the doors in the distance. "Keep waiting for someone to walk through that door. Not sure I want to hear what they have to say."

"Scarlet's strong. She'll fight her way through this."

Roman pushed to his feet, pacing the length of the room. "She took two bullets point blank to the shoulder. Fuck, did you see how much blood she'd lost?"

"It was hard to miss. But that doesn't mean she can't make it. Have faith." He stood, moving in beside him as Roman stared out a window. "I'm sensing something's changed between you two. Long week?"

Roman closed his eyes, remembering the soft give of her ass and the warm, wet slide of her sex. How she whispered her easy acceptance of him, kissing him as if she'd been waiting for the chance as long as he had. "You could say that."

Aiden released a long sigh. "I'm not blind, Roman. Or naïve. You were worried being that close to her, posing as her lover, would push you too far. I'm thinking it didn't quite push you enough. If you two became lovers, and I'm pretty damn sure you did, it didn't seem to give you the answers you've been looking for. You still seem...divided."

Roman glanced at the man. "Aiden, I..."

"Hey. I didn't tag along so I could judge. Or preach. You've always been up front about your love for Scarlet. I knew that going in. And what we've had... I know you have feelings for me, too. And I think you're smart enough to figure out that you mean more to me than a guy who shares my bed at times."

Roman turned to fully face Aiden. "What exactly are you trying to say?"

"Just that maybe loving two people isn't such a bad thing. Especially if your partner shares your dilemma. You're not the only one who has feelings for that girl."

"Are you trying to tell me you're in love with Scarlet?"

"What I'm trying to say is that I'm well on my way." Aiden traced his hand back along Roman's jaw. "And completely there where you're concerned." He eased away. "Just…give it some thought. This doesn't have to tear you apart if you don't let it."

"Why didn't you tell me this before?"

"Because you weren't ready to hear it. Roman, buddy, you're not in or out of the closet. You're stuck permanently in the doorway. And this was too important for me to push you. I've never felt threatened by Scarlet. Hell, the girl's charm is infectious. Being around her and you this past year…" He shrugged. "What can I say? You two are a lot alike. You have a way of working under someone's skin. I was hoping you'd come to this conclusion on your own. That you'd see that the three of us could be amazing together. Unfortunately, you're extremely stubborn."

"I… Fuck. I don't even know what to say to that. How to get it all straight inside my head."

"Wrong head. And you might want to try using your heart."

Roman stared at Aiden, the familiar warm feeling billowing in his chest. Damn, Aiden was right. What he felt for Scarlet… Shit. It was mirrored in Aiden. And he'd been fooling himself if he thought he wasn't just as invested in Aiden as he was in the woman still fighting for her life.

Roman speared his hand through his hair, leaning his head against the wall when the far doors opened, a man dressed in scrubs and a flowing white lab coat slowly walking through. Roman pushed off the wall, meeting the man halfway. He clenched his jaw, preparing for the worst as the man nodded at him, releasing a long, slow breath.

The doctor smiled. "I'll go out on a limb and assume you're Detective Roman Kincaid?"

"How's Scarlet?"

"Woman's a fighter. She suffered extreme blood loss and sustained multiple fractures to her shoulder and lacerations of the surrounding tissues. Gave us all quite a scare. But we were able to stop the bleeding. Repaired most of the damage, though she'll probably need additional surgeries if she wants full mobility back in that joint."

Roman blinked, a strange ringing in his ears. "So, she's okay?"

"She'll be our guest for a while, but...there's no reason she shouldn't make a full recovery." He gave Roman a pat on the shoulder. "Get some rest. You don't look so good, yourself."

"When can I see her?"

"She's in recovery. And we're keeping her sedated for the next couple of days. Go home. Sleep. Or at least curl up on a couch somewhere."

Roman thanked the man, sinking into the nearest chair, as his strength just seemed to fade.

Aiden kneeled in front of him, tilting his head to snag his gaze. "Roman?"

"I thought I'd lost her."

"We. That *we'd* lost her."

Roman stared at the man. God, how could he be so sure? So at ease with his decision? With being attracted — hell, in love — with two people? Roman closed his eyes. Damn, he was tired.

Aiden squeezed his thigh. "You need to rest. Stop thinking for a few hours. You'll figure it out."

Roman nodded. He needed to sleep. Clear his head. He could decide his next move tomorrow, when he didn't feel completely lost. When his every thought wasn't centered on the fact his heart was bound to two people, and he had absolutely no idea what to do about it.

Chapter Three

Three months later…

Scarlet kneeled next to the body, staring at the letters carved into the woman's stomach. The marks were rough. Jagged. The killer's anger clearly etched in the deep gashes and repeated strikes.

April.

What the hell was that supposed to mean? And why did the girl's face look disturbingly familiar?

A man moved in beside her, his boots clicking to a halt. "Damn. That's not something you see every day. Whoever did this certainly has a lot of anger inside. Any idea who the woman is?"

Scarlet rose off the dirty warehouse floor, covering her mouth with the back of her hand against the stench. She shuffled over as the crime scene techs arrived, photographing everything in sight. "No wallet, no personal effects. Not even clothes to track down. We'll have to wait for forensics to give us a name. Her hands are intact. Should be able to get usable prints. Looks like she's had some work done, too. Those are implants. There should be serial numbers recorded on them we can track down if all else fails. But shit... I don't know about you, Bates, but I've never seen a body this tortured. Creeps me the hell out."

She glanced around the barren building, a shiver working down her spine. She hadn't been inside a place like this since...

She closed her eyes against the flood of memories, most too disjointed to be more than ghosted images in her head—images she'd rather forget. A group of men gathered beside a car. The echo of gunfire. Blood on Roman's shirt.

Roman. Fuck. She didn't want to remember him, either. She vaguely recalled him being in her recovery room—hearing him whisper words of love in her ear—before literally vanishing from her life. By the time she'd been fully coherent, he'd left with nothing more than a note saying he'd taken a position within the F.B.I. and that he'd contact her soon. That he needed time. Hell, time was a luxury none of them had, and the jackass had yet to do so much as send her a text.

She lifted her hand, rubbing her shoulder against the sudden ache that flared beneath her flesh. The rain and cold irritated the metal plates they'd used to help fuse her scapula back together, and just standing in the dank warehouse made her skin crawl.

Bates followed as she walked toward the doors. "You think this is an isolated incident?"

"We'd know if there'd been more bodies found in Seattle. Trust me. This kind of thing gets press time." She stopped, dragging her fingers through her hair. "Why April? That her name? The month? What the hell kind of message is that?"

"Beats the hell out of me."

Scarlet groaned, glancing back at the body. She should have stayed in narcotics. At least there, creeps only tried to kill her. They didn't leave cryptic messages carved in flesh. She shook her head, walking into the rain. Looked as if December was coming in like a lion.

* * * *

"Scarlet. Thanks for coming." The lieutenant motioned to the set of chairs opposite his desk. "Please, have a seat."

Scarlet walked into the man's office, cautiously claiming a chair, wondering who the others were for. It wasn't even six o'clock, the rest of the office empty save for a few diehards working on cases. The lieutenant had woken her thirty minutes ago, nothing but a guarded, 'you need to get over here', given as a reason for the meeting, and she couldn't stem the uneasy feeling prickling her skin with goosebumps. It wasn't like the man to be this mysterious. Lieutenant Richard Powell was a straight shooter. He called it as he saw fit and didn't care if his decisions were politically correct. He lived for the job. Period.

The man gave her a token smile, offering her a cup of coffee. "Three sugars, right?"

She nodded, accepting the Styrofoam cup. "Hasn't changed in the ten years I've been at the precinct."

"Ten years that have taken you from a beat cop to narcotics and now homicide. That's a pretty distinguished record."

"Helps when you don't really have a personal life."

"Right. Because it has nothing to do with the fact you've worked your ass off."

She gave him a tight smile. "Thanks. Though I doubt you dragged my butt out of bed to give me a cup of coffee and stroke my ego."

"Wish I had." He broke eye contact, shuffling through some papers on his desk.

Scarlet groaned inwardly. The man's actions didn't bode well. It meant she wasn't going to like whatever he had to say. Though, she'd assumed that from the start.

She leaned forward, catching his gaze as he looked up at her. "Just spit it out."

He huffed. "I must be getting old if you're reading me that easily. And what happened to my very presence instilling fear?"

"I've spent three months recovering from a bad night. Watching you brood isn't so scary."

His expression softened. "How is the shoulder? If it's too soon for you to be back here…"

"I'm fine. Aches when it rains, but I'll manage. And staying home was driving me crazy. Not sure how people do it."

Of course, if she'd had Roman to help pass the time…

She cursed the treacherous thought, telling that voice in her head to bugger off. The man would have called by now if he'd had any thoughts other than that making love to her had been a mistake, even if it had been in the line of duty. Either way, he'd obviously moved on. Escaped.

Powell eased back in his chair, tossing a folder on the desk in front of her.

She raised an eyebrow, reaching for it when he placed his palm over top.

"Before you look at those, I want you to know we'll do everything within our power to keep you safe."

"Keep me safe? Now you are scaring me."

She waited for him to remove his hand before opening the file, staring at the photos stuck inside. Her chest tightened at the sight, a numbing haze slowly blanketing her. Three other women, all carved with the same slashing strokes—each one with a different month inscribed on her abdomen.

Scarlet closed her eyes. Damn, she knew she'd recognized the girl. But with all the dirt and grime—blood splattered over most of the woman's skin—she hadn't been able to tell for sure.

She looked up, her heart beating a tattoo against her ribs. "So this wasn't the first victim."

It wasn't a question and the lieutenant merely shook his head. "I only wish it was. Three others in varying parts of the country. Seems whoever's behind this is tracking them down, regardless of the distance—killing them wherever he finds them. Ms. April was in Seattle as part of a convention." He paused for a moment, sighing. "And I know you recognize their faces and names. They were all part of that photo shoot you and Roman infiltrated a few months back for Spyce Magazine."

Scarlet nodded, not sure what to say, as she let the folder fall to the desk, stalking to her feet and moving roughly to the window. She carded her hand through her hair, leaning against the wall for support. "So what now? You pulling me off the investigation because my name's on his shit list? And don't lie to me. We both know I'm on that list, even if it's at the end."

"The fact you were Ms. December as part of your cover is exactly why you're in here."

Scarlet scowled when a knock sounded on the door. She turned, her breath stalling as she stared into a set of stunning blue eyes.

The guy smiled, bracing one arm against the doorframe as he nodded at her. "Hey, Scarlet. Heard you were back at work. It's good to see you."

She opened her mouth, quickly closing it when nothing came out but a raspy breath. Aiden Cross. Roman had introduced them a year ago, and Aiden had fit in flawlessly. He'd become part of her small circle of friends ever since—until the shooting. He'd pulled the same disappearing act Roman had, leaving another void in her life. She hadn't realized how much she cared for Aiden until she'd lost him—that somewhere along the line she'd developed feelings far greater than just friendship. God, she'd even made a pass at the man once after a particularly hard case and far too many tequilas. But he'd never mentioned it, and she'd been too embarrassed ever to confront him.

Aiden sighed, looking as if he was reluctant to come any closer. "I suppose I have some explaining to do."

The way he broke eye contact, kicking at the floor, a slight flush coloring his cheeks, sent a cold shiver down her spine. Fuck. She hadn't stopped to consider that Aiden had been avoiding her because of Roman. That there was something more between the men than friendship. Though she'd wondered on a few occasions—with their easy comfort and physical contact—but the way Roman had touched her—worshiped her body despite the circumstances—she hadn't considered...

She took a shuddered breath as pieces started falling into place, leaving a hole larger than any bullet.

Powell cleared his throat. "Perhaps we should all have a seat."

Scarlet fisted her hands at her sides, glaring at Aiden. "Perhaps Special Agent Cross should explain what the hell he's doing here when he hasn't given a fuck in three months?"

Aiden's mouth pulled tight, and he stalked halfway toward her before seemingly reining in his control. "That's not true. I was at the hospital."

"When? While I was unconscious? Thanks for the show of support, buddy. Glad I at least know who my friends are, now."

The man's jaw clenched, the vein in his temple pulsing. "We're far more than friends, but this isn't the time or the place for that conversation. I'd hoped to meet with you privately before something like this cropped up, but then you had the displeasure of finding that body. And now we're left scrambling to get a handle on this shit."

"What has that dead girl got to do with you?"

"As I'm sure the lieutenant mentioned, the bastard responsible for these murders crossed state lines — more than once. Unfortunately, the distance between them kept it off our radar until they found Ms. March. We were called in a few days ago. Were just piecing together his timeline when we got word of the fourth victim." He shook his head. "I've never seen anyone kill like this. The aggression. The obvious torture."

"So you brought me in here to what? Scare me? Tell me this is federal case? You could have sent me a memo and avoided this."

Powell stepped over to her. "No one's trying to scare you. Now sit, before I have to send you both to a corner for a time out."

Scarlet huffed, taking the seat farthest from the door as Aiden sat two away from her. He glanced her way, openly measuring her before grunting and looking away, boot still kicking at the floor. A tight feeling constricted her chest, but she let her anger and pain soothe the ache.

Powell waited until he was sure he had their attention before focusing on her. "As you've guessed, the large scope of this investigation has brought it under federal jurisdiction. However, our friends in the F.B.I. have met with a few roadblocks with respect to the other models."

"Roadblocks?" Scarlet grimaced. "Just show them the damn crime scene photos. I guarantee you those girls will be lining up for protective services."

"It's not the ladies that are refusing to help us." Powell motioned to Aiden. "Perhaps you should fill her in on the rest."

Scarlet glared at Aiden. "By all means. Explain the situation, Agent Cross."

Aiden's mouth quirked, the blue color of his eyes deepening. "Good to see your recent brush with death hasn't tamed that wild side of yours. Fine. When we realized that this sicko was systematically hunting the women from that photo shoot, we immediately contacted the representatives at Glade Manor. Requested a list of all of the women's real names and addresses. I'm sure it's not surprising that we were met with some...resistance."

Scarlet groaned. "Let me guess. If the press gets word of some serial killer murdering Glade's models—by month, no less—it could financially ruin his magazine."

"The guy's lawyers rattled off a bunch of legal speak, which basically reduced to one major hitch—all the models signed confidentiality contracts. That means that Glade doesn't have to release their names to anyone short of a court order."

"And because you can't prove this list even exists..."

"We can't get a judge to sign off on it. And by the time we do, God knows how many more of these women will be dead."

Scarlet sighed. "Is there a silver lining to this cloud?"

"Sort of." Aiden glanced at Powell then back at her. "You're aware that after the bust, the Seattle Police department was able to slap an injunction on Glade, preventing him from publishing those original photos? Used the guise of evidence to protect your identity."

"A small gesture that made getting shot somewhat bearable."

Aiden's jaw tensed, his gaze narrowing on her before he continued. "Right. Anyway, Glade decided that he'd circumvent the decision by having all the women come back and do another shoot—one the police couldn't take from him. Turns out they'd already photographed the four dead girls a few weeks ago. Couldn't believe they'd been murdered."

"Please tell me that swayed their decision to release the other names."

"Not quite. But Glade was willing to forgo his previous schedule and assemble all the remaining models at his mansion for a retreat over the next three weeks. Give us time to track this guy down without having the women at risk. Or at least, that's what the man believes. No amount of talking can convince him that whoever's behind this won't let this retreat stop him. That he'll crash it."

"Can't you force his hand?"

"With what? We can't prove these women are in danger. We don't have a viable reason to get a warrant, other than the possibility they might be on some kind of list we can't be sure exists. Glade isn't under investigation. We have no legal right to be at his estate."

"Four women are dead, Aiden. I think that's a pretty strong indicator."

"Don't preach to the choir, baby. I'm on your side."

Scarlet let her head loll back, hoping the ache between her eyes wasn't an indication of how the rest of the day would play out. She glanced at Aiden. "So why the meeting? Sounds as if your hands are tied, which means there's nothing we can do, either."

He looked at Powell and something passed unspoken between them. She straightened, moving her focus between them. That voice in her head was talking again, and she didn't like what it had to say.

"Except for the part where he's having the remaining models attend his retreat."

She pushed to her feet as pieces starting clicking into place. "No."

Aiden rose beside her, quickly closing the distance between them. "Scarlet. I know you don't want to hear this, but...you're all we have. Glade thinks the Feds are working the case. Trying to find the killer while he keeps all his pretty little playmates safe inside that fortress of his. But we all know some walls and a few muscle heads aren't going to keep these women from becoming the killer's next target. Everything in this man's profile suggests he'll take whatever risks are necessary to continue his spree. Hell, our profilers think this guy is somehow connected to that magazine. That he probably already has access. That's how he was able to track down the first four women immediately following their shoot. We need someone on the inside. Someone who won't raise suspicions." He took a step closer, invading her space. "Someone who's been invited to attend."

A dull roar sounded in her head as the room dipped slightly. Aiden grabbed her arm, steadying her when she swayed on her feet. He mumbled at her to breathe before she shook off the strange sensation, pulling out of his hold. She took a few stumbling steps away, palming the wall as she forced in a series of quick breaths, willing her heart to slow.

Powell darted out from behind his desk, stepping over to stand beside her. Concern etched the creases in his forehead as he watched her breathe. "Scarlet..."

"I didn't receive an invitation."

"You did. It came yesterday to the PO Box we'd set up as Ms. December's address."

"But... Don't ask me to become her again. You have no idea what it was like...all those cameras. The outfits that didn't even cover me. Men staring at my ass as if it was theirs if they wanted it."

"I know this must be upsetting to you."

"Upsetting? I've been back six weeks and I've spent more time pulling copies of my naked ass off every bulletin board in the damn station than I have chasing down murders! Hell, Lucas and James are using one as their bloody screen saver. I've worked too hard to get where I am just to become a piece of meat the men in this station think they can stare at."

The lieutenant chuckled as she glanced back at him over her shoulder. "You could take that as a compliment, Detective. You've got one hell of a cute ass."

"Not funny." She sighed, looking back out of the window. December used to be her favorite month. Now it was just a name she wanted to forget.

Aiden shouldered up beside her, giving her a gentle nudge. "You know we wouldn't be asking if we weren't desperate. But we've only got three weeks left before the year's up. And this creep isn't going to let this drag out into January. He wants those women dead. And like it or not, you're on that list."

Images flashed through her head again, the memories stinging her eyes. She swiped angrily at the few that slipped free, refusing to look at either man. How did she explain parading around in bikinis and fuck-me-boots was only part of the issue? That reviving the memories of what she and Roman had shared was what really scared her, and she just didn't know if she could be that woman again. She looked up, glancing from Aiden over to the lieutenant and back.

Powell gave her a reassuring smile. "Regardless of what the Feds want, I won't order you to take the job. Not if your mind's not in it."

"I already told you. I'm fine." She rubbed her hands along her arms, wondering when it had gotten so cold. "Look. Even if I wanted to do this, there's no way I can go back there. Not after the shooting. My cover—"

"Was never revealed." Aiden sidestepped, filling her view. "Trust me. We checked. Glade doesn't have a clue you're really a cop. He thought you were like that other blonde at the drop sight. Wrong place. Wrong time. Our cover story that Everett was exploiting women held. As far as anyone at that magazine is concerned, you're just a sexy cover model. Period."

"Even if that's true. This isn't your conventional manor. Everyone that goes there does so as a couple. Or a threesome or a quartet if that's how you swing. Glade doesn't care. All he cares is that every woman shows up with at least one lover. In his warped brain, it justifies all those sex games he makes his guests play. You don't have to interact with others because you already have a mate. But if you do…it's consensual. That's how Roman was able to shadow my every move." She released a ragged breath, hating the fact they both knew she was more than shaken. "And you have to participate or you get kicked out. Simple as that. I went that first time because I trusted Roman with more than my life. With him gone..."

Aiden glanced at the lieutenant over his shoulder then back at her. "About that..."

The soft press of boots whispered across the room a moment before a voice sounded off to her right. "Hello, Scarlet."

She turned, her breath lodged tight, eyes locked on his. Her heart kicked twice as she pushed past the other men and stalked toward him, slapping the sexy smile off his face. "You fucking bastard!"

Roman took a step back, his hands braced for another attack. "Now, darling, I can..."

"Don't 'darling' me. Three months, Roman. Three months! The last thing I remember is you carrying me out of that warehouse. Then I woke up two weeks later with a couple of bullets for souvenirs and a letter saying you'd joined the Feds. No call, no email...not so much as a fucking text since then." She shook out her hand, clenching her jaw to keep the sudden rush of tears at bay. "After two years as partners, you owed me more than that. And god knows we were much more than partners."

Roman shuffled his feet, brushing his fingers along his jaw as he shot the other men a desperate glance. "You're right. It was a dick move and I deserve far more than a slap in the face. Now, if you'd just stop being mad for one minute, I can explain—"

"Save it. Any explanation is three months overdue."

A throat cleared behind her and she spun, crossing her arms on her chest as Roman's scent drifted over to her. She cursed under her breath as her nipples tightened and her pussy wept simply from breathing in the spicy aroma. Hell, just seeing him had made her treacherous heart leap for joy, resurrecting the broken pieces she'd buried inside.

Lieutenant Powell made his way over, nodding at her hand. "Feel any better?"

"He deserved it."

"No argument here. And seeing as he's a Fed..." The man smiled. "I realize this is a lot to take in. And if there were other options, I'd tell these boys to fuck off, myself. But..."

"But your hands are tied, and the Feds are breathing down the commissioner's neck. So he's passing his concern on to you." She nodded. "I get it. And if you want me to reincarnate Ms. December, I will."

The tension eased from the man's shoulders. "I knew you'd do us proud. Now I suggest you head home, pack some stuff. I've already had your clothes and items from the previous mission pulled from inventory. I'll have Roman and Aiden bring them when they come to pick you up in an hour—"

"Whoa. Back the bunny wagon up a second. What do you mean Roman and Aiden?"

Powell glanced at the two men. "After what happened last time, and with a serial killer likely stalking you, personally, we can't send just two of you in there." He snorted. "Not that three is that much better but...I'm not risking your life."

Her jaw hinged open, and all she could do was stand there, staring at the two men.

Powell sighed. "Scarlet. It's for your own safety. And Roman assured me you trusted Aiden—"

"You suggested this?" She turned to face Roman, hands on her hips. "Why the hell didn't anyone ask me? I'm the one parading around in tit tassels and a bloody thong. The one who's going to have to convince everyone that you're both my lovers. Why…"

She gasped when Roman lunged at her, backing her into the wall. He pressed his body tight to hers, the sheer size of him stealing her breath. She could feel every twitch of his muscles as he palmed the wall behind her, one hand beside her head, the other grazing her hip. But it was the hard ridge against her stomach that dipped the room as he leaned in, his breath mixing with hers.

He tilted his head, not allowing her to break eye contact. "Damn it, Scarlet, are you seriously going to stand there and tell me you don't trust Aiden with your life? Because despite everything, you've never lied to me before. Hell of a time to start now."

She shifted her focus to Aiden as he moved in behind Roman's shoulder, obscuring what was left of the room. His gaze locked on hers as if daring her to deny Roman's claim. She let her head connect with the wall, nothing more than a muted whisper of air passing her lips.

Roman drew a deep breath, his expression softening slightly. "I know you're mad—and hurt. But I'm not putting your life at risk because of that. I let you down once. Not going to happen again."

His words echoed in her head as he eased back, taking two long strides away. Aiden moved with him, standing next to Powell. Did Roman really blame himself for the shooting? Was that why he'd stayed away?

The lieutenant scanned the group, shaking his head as he returned to his desk, placing his hip on the edge. "We good?"

Scarlet inhaled, doing her best to gather even a modicum of composure. Shit, what was it about those two men that unraveled her? Reduced her to nothing more than fiery need? She looked away, wishing she'd stayed in bed this morning. "I'd like all the files on the murders put onto a tablet for me. The old case, too. It'll give me a chance to go over it on the ride there, seeing as Glade has a strict policy on no cellular devices at his mansion. God forbid someone steals his thunder and releases the next cover spread early. Roman can bring it with him when he and Aiden pick me up."

Powell nodded. "Consider it done. Anything else?"

"Just this." She swung her gaze over to Roman again. "I'm doing this because I don't want those women's blood on my hands. Don't assume it means you're forgiven. I might have to work with you two, but I don't have to like it." She bit her lip to keep it from quivering as she spun on her heels and marched down the hall. She'd play their game, but they were in for one hell of a surprise if they thought she'd let them back inside her heart.

Chapter Four

Special Agent Aiden Cross watched Scarlet storm out of the office, head held high, mouth pursed to keep those tears in her eyes from spilling over, and he knew they'd more than fucked up. While he'd suspected Scarlet would be angry, hurt—he hadn't expected her to look at them as if they'd betrayed her.

He glanced at Roman, reading the man's thoughts by the press of his lips. He knew Roman blamed himself. After Scarlet had confessed her love—Roman had pulled away. Distanced himself from everything. Everyone. He couldn't seem to get past the fact he'd allowed her to be shot. That he hadn't protected her when she'd needed him most. It didn't matter that Aiden had tried to justify her sacrifice—that it was a partner's right to make that choice. All Roman could see was her blood on his hands. Her life slowly slipping away in his arms.

They'd spent the first two weeks glued to her side until the moment she'd fluttered her eyelids open, and Roman had bolted. He'd accepted the job Aiden had offered months previous and cut himself off from his old life. They'd spent the next few weeks just talking as friends before they'd found their way back as lovers, reigniting a passion that never failed to take Aiden's breath away. But the harder they fell, the more they both realized something was missing. *Someone*. Hell, he'd finally convinced Roman to grow some balls and just knock on Scarlet's door when the calendar murders had been dumped on their desk. And they'd been rocked to the core.

It hadn't taken much to picture their girl posed in some alleyway, stripped bare, her body tortured. Broken. They'd lobbied for two days to take lead, finally convincing Langley when Scarlet's name had appeared on the fourth murder investigation as the head detective. And once they'd confirmed her alter ego had remained intact, they'd moved forward with their operation. One that would either bind them together in a way they'd only dreamed of, or destroy them.

Lieutenant Powell whistled, chuckling when both men turned to look at him. He shook his head, giving them both a knowing grin. "Damn, but she's mad. I don't envy you boys the next couple of days. Going to be mighty cold in that oversized king bed with her like that. You'd best play nice until she forgives you or you might spend the entire mission taking turns sleeping in the bathtub." He chuckled again. "Of course, the fact she's in love with at least one of you, if not both, certainly puts the odds in your favor."

Aiden snapped his head toward Roman, unable to talk around the lump in his chest.

Roman took a step closer, his expression fixed. "Excuse me?"

Powell tsked. "Now who's lying? Please, give me some credit. I've known you for a dozen years. Scarlet nearly as long. And I've spent the past two years watching you two through that glass. You were smitten with the girl the moment I made her your partner. And you've been falling in love with each other every day since." He glanced at Aiden. "And she wouldn't be sparring with you that way if she didn't care. I'm guessing your friendship has...progressed without either of you actually acknowledging it."

Roman released an audible breath. "Well...this is awkward."

Powell waved Roman's words away. "You're not the first partners to fall in love. Hell, all do, it's always just a tossup as to whether it's the kind where you punch each other in the shoulder and help get them laid or if you're the one taking your partner to bed." He raised an eyebrow. "I'm guessing that playing the role of lovers at the mansion pushed you two over the edge?" He merely nodded. "Explains why you left like you did, no offense to the Feds."

Aiden held up his hands. "None taken. But I can't say I'm upset that he decided to make the switch."

"I imagine not." Powell crossed his arms on his chest. "So level with me. You boys honestly think you can both pose as her lovers and not have it blow up in your faces? Knowing the lifestyle you'll be submersed in? What the three of you might have to do to maintain your cover? Roman? You don't strike me as the kind of guy who shares. Aiden, either."

Roman glanced at Aiden, silently asking him how much he wanted revealed. Aiden smiled. Fuck. He hadn't thought Roman would feel comfortable acknowledging the intimate side of their relationship. Not here. Not yet.

Powell groaned. "Ah, fuck. I'm an idiot. Does Scarlet know?"

Roman matched the man's stance. "That Aiden and I are lovers? She has a pretty damn good idea. Does she know I'm not the only man in love with her? That might take her by surprise. Though she'd be lying to herself if she thinks she doesn't have feelings for Aiden, as you've already pointed out."

Powell nodded. "Don't take this the wrong way, but...while I realize these are unique circumstances, what with the type of undercover work you might be required to perform... Are you sure this is wise? You boys seem a bit too close to be...objective."

"Generally, I'd agree. But in this instance..." Aiden ran a hand through his hair. "The very basis of this assignment is convincing everyone there we're involved. Intimately. The fact we have feelings for each other... It's Scarlet's life on the line if we don't pull this off. And she has to trust us. Regardless of what occurs inside those walls. Know that we won't let anyone hurt her, make her feel anything less than safe, no matter what's happening or who's watching."

"Sounds like you have your work cut out for you after reading hers and Roman's reports." Powell moved behind his desk. "I'll have that tablet and Ms. December's belongings ready within the hour. I've been informed that the Feds will be dealing with any correspondence, since we won't be able to simply call or text you. They've assured me they'll use appropriate measures to ensure your covers remain intact. With any luck, you three will catch this sick bastard before he strikes again."

"We'll do our best." Aiden turned then glanced back at the lieutenant. "We know how important this operation is, and I promise we won't do anything to put Scarlet's life at risk."

"See that you don't. Just watch your backs. You're pretty much on your own in there."

"There's always the chance this guy won't be able to get inside."

"Right. And we all believe that." Powell leaned back in his chair. "Oh, and, gentlemen… Tread lightly where Scarlet's concerned. She's still dealing with the fallout from that original case. And it'd be a shame for her to permanently damage anything…important… before you even get there."

Roman smiled. "We'll keep that in mind. We'll be in touch."

Aiden followed his lover out, hating the silence that stretched between them as they headed for their truck. He could tell by the stiff line of Roman's back and the way he clenched and released his hands at his sides that the man wasn't happy with Scarlet's reaction.

He waited until Roman slipped into the driver's side before turning and placing his hand over Roman's as he slid the keys into the ignition. Roman sighed, glancing at him before collapsing against the seat, staring at the ceiling as if it held some kind of magical answer.

He shook his head. "Did you see the look on her eyes? Fuck, that wasn't anger. That was pain. Betrayal."

Aiden twisted so he could better face the man. "Can't say I'm that surprised. She's right. She deserved better."

"Not helping."

"Would you rather I lie to you?"

Roman spared him a quick glance. "You could cushion the truth a bit."

59

"Sorry, buddy, not my style. Not when I'd be as pissed as she is if I were in her place. She lost both of us without so much as a satisfactory explanation. We knew the road back into her heart wouldn't be easy."

"What if there isn't a way? What if I just fucked up the one chance we had at being happy, all because I couldn't fucking think past my own fears? Shit, I should have just told her that day she woke up."

"We both know why you didn't. And despite everything, she's still in love with you. It's written across her face. Why do you think she's so upset? She cares."

"The girl has a hell of a memory—and temper. Neither is going to help us win her back."

"Nothing worth fighting for is ever simple."

Roman exhaled, allowing his head to bow toward his chest. The man looked as broken as Aiden knew he felt.

Aiden gave his thigh a squeeze. "We'll work this out. Promise."

"She's on that list, Aiden. If we don't catch his sorry ass, he'll kill her. And it'll be on us."

"Not going to let that happen. Period. Besides, she's not an easy target. She's trained, fights like a damn badger and is one hell of a good shot."

"Hard to hide a gun in the clothes she'll have to wear." He scrubbed a hand down his face. "She can't be left alone. Ever. Not even for a minute."

"Not my first rodeo. Yours or hers, either. We'll get this creep. Now start the damn truck. We only have an hour to get everything ready before we pick up her stuff then her. And it'd be rude to keep the lady waiting."

Roman revved the engine, heading out of the empty lot. They went through the motions, gathering supplies before heading back to the precinct. Powell met them with a suitcase of Ms. December's belongings and a tablet, not so subtly reminding them this was a joint endeavor and to keep him informed. Then they'd headed to Scarlet's, parking in front of the small bungalow she owned. Roman sat in the seat, staring at the front door for five minutes before Aiden punched him on the shoulder.

"You've been here a thousand times. She probably already knows we're out here. Now, we just look like fucking stalkers. Just man the hell up, already."

Roman glared at him. "Fuck you."

"Anytime. Anywhere, buddy. But it's not me you have to convince." He pointed at the door. "She'll understand, Roman. She might be angry for a while, standoffish. Hell, I'll considerate it lucky if we only have to grovel at her feet — but she'll forgive you. Us. That's what love's about. Now, go. I'm right behind you."

Roman huffed, slamming the door before striding up the walkway. He pounded on the door, palming the wall as he waited, muttering under his breath. Aiden smiled. Roman always was an extreme kind of guy. But that was part of his charm.

Scarlet yanked open the door, glaring at them as she crossed her arms on her chest. She wore a form-fitting red dress with a matching velvet shawl and thigh-high boots. The outfit hugged every damn curve of her body, highlighting her firm breasts and sexy ass. Aiden forced himself to swallow. Shit, he'd thought she looked hot in jeans and a tee. Dressed like this — the girl would turn more than a few heads.

She scowled at both of them, tapping her leather-booted foot on the floor. "You don't have to break the damn thing down, especially since you've been sitting out there just staring at the house." She grabbed a purse off a side table to her right and a small bag from the floor as she pushed past Roman.

Aiden snagged her arm, careful not to grip too tightly. "I thought you were going to pack?"

Scarlet looked at him, glancing at where he held her arm, but she didn't try to pull away. "I did." She held up the bag. "This is it."

"One bag? I thought women took everything they owned with them?"

She smiled sweetly at him. "I'm going to Glade Manor. That means I'll basically be naked for the foreseeable future. This dress is the least revealing outfit I'll wear until we close this case. I didn't need much."

Her words hit his gut. Shit. In all the planning, he hadn't stopped to really consider what she'd have to endure. How being on display might affect her. Not really.

He shifted in front of her, brushing his thumb along her cheek, keeping his other hand gently holding her arm. "I'm sorry. If there was any other way to get inside…"

Scarlet's expression softened, uncertainty creasing her forehead. She looked over at Roman, the lines deepening. "I…" She shrugged. "I know what's on the line. I'll deal."

Aiden nodded, unsure what else to say as she moved past them, climbing into the back of the truck. He glanced at Roman, but the man merely motioned him forward. Aiden walked to the vehicle, debating whether to ride with Roman in the front or sit with Scarlet in the back. Roman shook his head, pointing to the front. Aiden sighed. They needed to bridge the gap, and soon, or no one would believe they were friends, let alone lovers.

Roman started off the trip trying to broach the obvious distance between them, only to have Scarlet cut off his efforts by channeling her attention toward the tablet. They'd continued in silence, the miles slowly passing as a constant hum of the tires on the road. Snow dotted the landscape as they climbed into the mountains, nothing but evergreens blurring past the windows. Scarlet barely uttered a word, simply nodding when Roman went over the cover story, adding a reluctant yes here and there. She seemed determined to keep them at arm's length, her body language clearly conveying her displeasure at the situation. Roman stopped a couple of hours later at the gates to the estate, looking at her in the rear-view mirror as he waited for the bars to open.

It took a few moments before she glanced up, frowning as she caught his stare. "Problem?"

Roman snorted. "Just that we're here and you've hardly said two words to us since we picked you up, despite our efforts to contrary."

"I thought the purpose of this mission was to catch a serial killer?"

"It is. But we'd like a chance to talk first—to explain."

"Short of both of you being abducted by aliens, I don't want your explanation. I'm here to work. Which is why I've been going through the files. I can't bring the damn tablet into the retreat, thanks to Glade's paranoia. And I'd rather not end up as a chalk outline on some warehouse floor with the word *December* carved in my skin."

The vein in Roman's temple pulsed. "Do you honestly think Aiden and I are going to let that happen? Give us some credit, darling."

She huffed at his endearment. "Doesn't hurt to be prepared."

"Reading all those files isn't going to help us when we don't get past the damn doormen because we can't convince them we're together. And based on that permanent scowl on your face, no one's going to believe that."

Scarlet graced them with a stunning smile. "Oh, don't worry, baby. I'll be sweet as sugar to you boys whenever we're outside our room—every inch the doting lover I'm expected to be."

Roman grunted, driving through the entrance and up the winding driveway. Aiden knew Scarlet's continued distance cut Roman deep, but it wasn't something they could avoid. They'd created the unrest between them. They couldn't expect Scarlet to simply welcome them home, especially when they'd been thrust into such a volatile situation before they'd had a chance to work things out. Though if the girl thought she was going to win just because she could hold a grudge, she had a hard lesson ahead of her.

Roman parked the truck, twisting to face them. "Are we clear on the details of our relationship?"

Scarlet sighed. "I know the cover story. You went over it a dozen times." She scoffed at him. "Just because I didn't talk much doesn't mean I wasn't listening. It's my ass on the line. I'm not going to screw anything up."

"The bastard's going to have to go through me and Aiden if he wants you. Simple as that. Now are you sure you're ready? If you think it's too soon..."

Her bottom lip quivered for a moment as she grazed a hand across her shoulder. A hint of the girl bled through her façade before she drew herself up, every bit the confident woman they'd fallen in love with. "I said I could do this, and I will."

"Not really an answer but..." He looked out of the window as one of Glade's staff stepped up to the door, grabbing the rear handle. "Show time."

Scarlet plastered on an exuberant smile, accepting the man's hand as she exited the truck. Her heels clicked on the pavement as she took a few steps, waiting for Roman and Aiden to each take a side. She linked arms with them, giving each man a picture-perfect smile before matching their stride as they headed for the main doors.

Roman glanced at him, all but rolling his eyes. Damn, she was good. Not a trace of the disdain she'd been shooting their way evident in her expression or the way she carried herself. She moved easily within their grasp, leaning into Aiden when he palmed her back, guiding her through the door Roman held it open for them. Every sway of her hips echoed in Aiden's groin, spiking his dick against his zipper.

He leaned close to her ear as she swayed his way. "Scarlet. If you keep brushing against me like that..."

She didn't answer, just managed to graze her knuckles across his cock, allowing them to linger just long enough his damn dick hardened further against her touch. He saw a smile tease the corner of her mouth as she nodded to a couple off to her right. Fuck, she was going to kill them, and she didn't need a weapon to succeed.

Thomas Glade stood several yards away, greeting his guests as they made their way inside. Aiden scanned the room, groaning inwardly. He'd hoped

Glade would restrict the retreat to the women involved in their case, but apparently, the man didn't have an ounce of common sense. He'd turned the gathering into a goddamn gala, with a seemingly endless stream of people moving freely through the rooms.

Roman shouldered up beside him, smiling and nodding as he leaned in. "Can you believe this? There has to be upwards of fifty people just in this area alone. How the hell are we supposed to make anywhere secure?"

"We'll adapt. Just keep smiling."

Scarlet gave Aiden a light elbow, motioning to Glade with her head. Aiden sighed, following her lead as she made her way over to the man, accepting his embrace.

He stepped back, holding her hands as his gaze ran the length of her body. "Ms. December. I'd recognize you anywhere. And what a stunning vision in red."

Scarlet blushed as if on cue, affectionately palming her hand on the older man's arm. "Thomas, you are such a charmer. You remember Roman Kincaid, my lover and personal agent."

Thomas extended his hand, shaking Roman's. "Glad you could make it. Hope the snow didn't slow you down."

"It's a lovely drive." Roman turned to Aiden. "As mentioned on our reply to your generous invitation, we have a new partner. Thomas Glade, this is Aiden Cross."

Thomas eyed Aiden, accepting his hand. "A third. How intriguing." Glade leaned in closer. "I *am* correct in assuming you're more than just a pretty face to these two, aren't I?"

Scarlet laughed, effortlessly moving into Aiden's embrace, one arm wrapped around his waist as the other caressed his chest. "Do I look like a fool?"

She laughed again, the sound so fucking natural Aiden damn near laughed with her. Shit, she had Glade hanging on her every word.

She tsked Thomas. "What woman in her right mind would pass up a chance to have this in her bed? Especially when her lover wants him, too?"

Glade grinned. "What a wonderful development. As I recall, you two were rather timid the last time you were here. We were beginning to think you might be...plants."

Scarlet tensed ever so slightly, before she batted her eyelids, giving the man a roll of her eyes. "Funny. I heard the same thing about Ms. February. Will she be joining us?"

Glade's demeanor changed. "I'm afraid she can't be with us."

"Shame. Now, if you'll just inform us as to which room we'll be staying in..."

"East wing, last suite on the left." He cupped her elbow when she tried to walk past. "Our security requirements..."

"Our phones. How could I forget?"

She handed over her tablet and cell, still smiling at the man as Roman and Aiden followed suit.

Glade thanked them, not yet moving aside. "Not to sound suspicious, but... We're taking stricter precautions this time, what with that unfortunate incident involving Everett trying to exploit some of my girls. I'm sure you'll understand that it's for everyone's safety."

To her credit, Scarlet didn't even flinch. "Of course. What can we do?"

"It's quite simple, really. I'm just asking for every couple to offer a show of faith."

"Not sure I'm following you."

"Just a few minor things. First, all female guests must have at least one male escort with them at all times. No exceptions. Second, we expect every couple—or threesome in your case—to make an appearance at a few of our...engagements. Participation will be assumed, of course." Thomas glanced at Roman then Aiden. "And lastly, all guests are required to give a visual confirmation of their...involvement before being granted full access."

Scarlet took a step back, bumping into Aiden. He snagged her waist, cursing under his breath at the shiver that worked through her.

She recovered quickly, steadying her expression as she looked at Glade. "And how are we to achieve that?"

"Quite simply, my dear. Just give your lovers a kiss for me. Trust me. I've been in this business long enough to tell a real one from a fake." He snickered. "Unless you'd rather give us more of a show?"

Scarlet waved his suggestion away. "Can't start off the week with the grand finale. Every girl wants to have a bit of mystery about her."

"Touché. So a kiss it is."

Scarlet turned toward them, a momentary lapse of confidence creasing her brow. She opened her mouth just as Roman lunged forward, threading his fingers through her hair as he tugged her hard against his chest. She inhaled, her hands landing on his shoulders as he tipped her back slightly, crushing his mouth to hers. She made a muffled gasping sound before she melted against him, smoothing her fingers into his hair.

Roman commanded the kiss, every set of eyes stopping to stare at the couple as he made love to her mouth, licking and nibbling her bottom lip when he finally released her. Her eyes blinked open, the stunning blue far darker than they'd been moments before. He smiled down at her, easing her back up. She raised her hand to her chest, as she seemed to take a few labored breaths.

Aiden felt an answering tightness in his chest as Roman turned his gaze on him. Roman gave him a lift of an eyebrow before striking, taking Aiden's mouth in a demanding kiss. The man swept his tongue inside, a lingering hint of coffee adding to the heady flavor that was all Roman. Aiden answered in kind, using his added height to dominate Roman once he'd started to ease off. Aiden didn't hide his obvious arousal when he finally pulled back, knowing the hard line of his dick pressing against his pants would only add authenticity to their game.

Roman smiled, glancing at Scarlet as he stepped back. Her eyes were rounded in shock, her lips slightly parted as if she'd started to say something but hadn't remembered what it was.

Aiden took the opportunity to snag her around the waist, pulling her flush to his chest. He dipped down, nuzzling his lips against her neck. A hushed, "oh, God" murmured next to his ear as her breath hissed out on a sigh. He worked his way up her jaw, lifting both hands to cup her face as he brushed his lips across hers. A tremble shuddered through her as he slowly claimed her mouth, licking his way inside, humming at the sweet taste that burst on his tongue. She reminded him of chocolate and honey, with a distinctive tang that tempered the other flavors. Scarlet responded, following his retreat, tangling her tongue with his until he broke the kiss, holding her forehead to his. Their breath mixed, and he dropped another quick kiss on the corner of her mouth before gently releasing her, lowering his hands to her hips. Scarlet blinked, sucking in a few deep breaths before visibly drawing herself up, plastering on a smile as Thomas clapped his hands together.

He stepped between them, a sly grin on his face. "Well, well. Looks like we might have some new competition for some of our ruling champions. Because if you boys eat pussy and fuck half as good as you kiss, you'll give us all quite the show over the next couple of weeks." He bowed, waving them toward a sweeping staircase. "My staff has already taken your belongings up to your room. Feel free to take some time to recover from your trip. Festivities start first thing tomorrow. We'll send a schedule of the photo sessions to your room. I look forward to seeing much more of you three in the near future."

Aiden nodded. "Thanks. We'll see you soon."

He palmed Scarlet's back again, guiding her toward the staircase. She walked woodenly up the steps, barely registering the other people milling about as they made their way to their room. It wasn't until they'd locked it behind them that she seemed to snap back to her senses.

She whirled on them, hands on hips, anger coloring her features. "What the hell was that?"

Roman glanced at him, silently telling him to tread lightly. "You'll have to be a bit more specific. What was what?"

"That kiss."

Roman furrowed his brow. "It was what we needed to do to convince the old man we're exactly what we appear to be." He took a calculated step closer.

"Unless you wanted us to take option two and give him a real show."

She clenched her jaw, narrowing her gaze. "Not funny."

Aiden moved in beside Roman. "It's not like we had a choice. And if it means anything, you were very convincing."

"Me? It wasn't *me* that convinced him."

Hurt flashed in her eyes, and Aiden didn't miss the way she blinked away unshed tears. He looked at Roman but the man seemed equally confused.

Aiden shuffled closer, frowning when she crossed her arms defensively across her chest. "Scarlet? What's going on?"

"Maybe you boys should tell me."

"Tell you what?"

She kicked at the floor, shame hunching her shoulders, before glancing at them—the hurt impossible to miss this time. "You could start by telling me how long you two have been lovers. Because there's no way that kiss was the first you've ever shared."

Roman closed the distance, stopping when she took a few quick steps back. "Don't. Don't fucking back away like you think we'd ever do anything to hurt you."

"Oh, you mean like disappearing from my life with nothing more than a few token words?"

Roman faltered for a moment, guilt tightening the fine lines around his mouth. "I've tried talking to you—at the station and on the drive up, but you refuse to give me a chance to explain."

Scarlet swiped at her cheeks as a few tears slipped free, cringing as they fell silently to the floor. A mumbled curse crossed the short distance between them as she took what looked like a fortifying breath. "I think you just did." She spun on her heels, stalking to the bathroom before closing the door, the sound of the lock tumbling into place echoing through the room.

Roman crossed over to the door, palming the surface. "This isn't helping, Scarlet. We need to talk."

"I need some time."

He leaned his forehead against the door, looking completely lost. "Please. Darling. Just let us in."

"You and Aiden can take the bed."

Roman fisted his hand, huffing out a breath before straightening. "Fine. You need some time, we'll give you what we can, but you can't hide forever. And we're not going anywhere."

He walked out of the room, slamming the door behind him. Aiden headed for the bed, sinking down on the edge as he shucked his jacket off his shoulders, rolling them in an effort to ease the straining muscles. This definitely wasn't going as planned. He only hoped they reached an understanding before the killer struck again.

Chapter Five

Roman stood in the bathroom doorway, staring at Scarlet as she slept in the bathtub—a pillow and her hands tucked under her head, a single blanket tossed across her. She'd spent over an hour hiding in the plush en suite last night before filing out, grabbing her belongings as she'd turned back toward the room. She'd stopped and simply stood there, waiting while they'd used the facilities before closing the door again, this time leaving it unlocked.

Aiden had checked on her after midnight, spending the next thirty minutes sitting beside her, just watching her sleep. He hadn't spoken when he'd finally ventured to their bed, giving Roman a kiss before turning over and drifting off. Roman had tried to get some rest, but every damn noise had put him on edge, the lingering doubt of her safety nagging at him. Though his head told him there wasn't a way for anyone to get to her without walking through the room, his heart couldn't stand the distance. Couldn't ease without being able to reach behind him to feel her body curled next to him. This manor was the first time they'd shared a bed. And while he hadn't assumed she'd be happy about sharing one again, he hadn't considered she'd resort to sleeping in the damn tub.

She snuffled in her sleep, shifting slightly before quieting again. God, she was beautiful. The way her brown hair cascaded over her shoulders, forming loose curls around her face. Her long eyelashes rested against creamy skin, hiding the brilliant blue that always made him think of the ocean—bright when she was happy, dark and gray when she got angry. He loved her moody little quirks—the way she scrunched her nose up when she thought he'd lost his mind. Or how her smile lit up her entire face, as if she'd flicked on a switch. She'd always looked at him like that. At Aiden too. As if they made her happy in a way no one else could.

God, what he wouldn't do to get that back. To have her gaze at him with an emotion other than anger or sadness.

"Have I told you it's kind of creepy the way you're just standing there, staring at her?"

"You mean the way you did for thirty minutes last night?"

"Just wake her up. Gotta face the music sooner or later, buddy. Tick, tock."

Roman glanced over at Aiden, admiring the view. Chest bare, blond hair tousled about his head, he looked more than tempting. Of course, making love to the man was out of the question until they'd had a chance to talk to Scarlet. She'd seemed deeply hurt that they'd become lovers without her knowledge, and the last thing they needed was for her to walk in on them.

He closed his eyes. Just thinking about the three of them together, bodies writhing, skin gleaming in the bright sunlight, made his dick jerk inside his pants. He clenched his jaw, flipping off Aiden before moving farther into the bathroom. He wasn't sure he was up to another round of her glaring at them, or worse — watching her cry.

Shit, in the two years he'd known her, he'd never once seen her cry. Sure, she'd shed a few tears chopping onions, or watching some sappy chick flick, but somehow that didn't really count. Not like last night. The way she'd brushed them away, acting as if the simple act had weakened her somehow. It'd made him wonder in she'd cried others over the past three months. If he and Aiden had hurt her far worse than they'd ever imagined.

He pushed the ugly thoughts aside. He couldn't change what they'd done. He could only pray she'd find a way to forgive them. Allow them to spend the rest of their lives making it up to her. Showing her how perfect they were together. How much they loved her.

He kneeled next to the tub, brushing her hair off her forehead, enjoying the play of her skin beneath his fingers. It was so soft. So damn tempting. And knowing how sweet she'd taste, how wet she'd get, just tortured him more. He wanted her back.

He lowered his hand, easing the cover back slightly as he stared at her shoulder. Two raised scars marred her flesh, the angry welts barely healed. He knew if he ran his fingers along her blade, he'd feel the outline of every screw holding the plates in place. Her cost for saving his life.

Footsteps padded behind him. "It was her choice to make, just like it'd be yours or mine. You need to move past that. She doesn't blame you —"

"How do you know?"

"Because I saw the look on her face yesterday when you alluded to the idea you were the reason she got shot."

"I was. If she hadn't pushed me aside—"

"You'd be dead. Do you seriously think that would have hurt her less? That she regrets it?"

Roman sighed. "At this particular moment?"

Aiden chuckled. "Wanting to kick our asses isn't quite the same as actually wishing you were dead. And I'm pretty sure once she's made her point, the makeup sex is going to be more than worth it."

"Who says there'll be makeup sex?"

Roman snapped his head around, pinned by a set of perfectly blue eyes.

Scarlet pushed herself up, wincing a bit as her shoulder twisted slightly, before leaning against the tub. She tunneled her hand through her hair, tossing the mass of silky strands about her face, making her look every inch the wildcat he knew her to be. She cocked her head over, grinning at them. "But Aiden's right about one thing."

Roman glanced at the man then back to her. "What's that?"

"I'd like nothing more than to kick your ass. Both of you."

Roman spread his arms wide. "Right here, darling. Get your pretty ass out of that tub, and I'm all yours."

"What point is there in kicking your ass when you're ready for it? I'm not that nice. Trust me. You won't see it coming until it's too late."

"Suit yourself. We're not going anywhere."

She huffed at his words, the awkwardness between them returning. She sat in silence for a minutes before looking away. "What time is it?"

"Early."

She nodded. "Did they bring the schedule by? It'd be nice to know when I have to psych myself up to head out that door wearing mostly my smile."

"It's not as if we like this any more than you do."

"Of course not. Seeing as you two have to strip down...oh wait. That's just me."

Roman crossed his arms, tension straining his shoulders. "Do you really think we want all those slimy bastards gawking at you, wondering what it would be like fuck you?" He shook his head. "I thought you knew us better than that."

"Starting to wonder if I know you boys at all."

"Not fair, Scarlet. We..."

A knock sounded at the door. He straightened, motioning to Aiden as the man darted over to the dresser, removing his weapon. Scarlet cursed quietly, climbing out of the tub before gathering the pillow and blanket and carrying it back to the bed. She arranged it on top, making it look natural when the knock sounded again.

"Mr. Kincaid? It's Thomas Glade. Can I come in for a moment?"

"Shit. Get in the bed. Both of you and make it look as if he's interrupting us." Roman grabbed a towel, wrapping it around his waist to cover his boxers as he tossed his shirt aside. "Coming."

Scuffling noises sounded behind him, followed by a harsh gasp. He turned, missing a step as he took in the scene behind him. Aiden had stripped off Scarlet's T-shirt and tossed her on the bed. He'd positioned his body behind hers, one of his hands and his forearm covering her breasts. He'd draped the blanket low over their hips, making it more than apparent they were both naked beneath the covers.

Roman caught his balance, palming the handle as Aiden claimed Scarlet's mouth, her soft moaning rumbling free.

He opened the door, smiling at the older man waiting in the hallway. "Thomas. This is an unexpected surprise." We waved him inside. "Sorry for the delay. After all the traveling yesterday, we were just making up for some lost time."

Glade stepped inside, eyes widening as he watched Aiden slowly release Scarlet, keeping her body pressed tight to his. "By all means. Don't let me stop you."

Aiden eased Scarlet back, stilling covering strategic sections of her body with his. He glanced up, feigning surprise better than Roman had anticipated. "Didn't expect to be part of the show." He nuzzled Scarlet's neck. "She's the one worth watching."

Glade grinned. "I agree. She's lovely."

Roman stepped between Glade and the bed, allowing the man just a hint of the couple behind him. "Was there something we could help you with? Or are you just ensuring we got settled?"

Glade reached inside his sports jacket, removing a manila envelope with a set of papers stapled onto the corner. "This was delivered for Mr. Cross early this morning. Rather ingenious product. It apparently guards against tampering. Though some might assume that you're trying to hide something from us."

Roman accepted the offering, thumbing the pages as he motioned to Aiden. "We apologize for the intrusion on your retreat. Aiden owns a number of dojos, and he's in the midst of a merger. These are just legal papers, as you no doubt surmised from the return address. His lawyers are rather...particular when it comes to confidentiality. They also don't seem to believe in holidays. We'll do our best to keep any correspondence limited."

"Of course. I applaud a man who strikes out on his own. Builds his wealth from nothing. You mentioned dojos." Glade eyed the man. "Which discipline do you practice?"

Aiden shifted, somehow keeping Scarlet's breasts still covered. "Jujitsu. Though I like to dabble with mixed fighting — just for fun."

"What an interesting career choice. I took the liberty of including Scarlet's photography schedule as well as a list of other activities." Glade let his gaze drift the length of Scarlet's body, lingering where the blanket gave just a teasing glimpse of the hollow of her hips, where her abdomen joined the top of her mound. "Let me know if you need to send any faxes or the like. I'll inform my staff that they're to bring any deliveries straight to your door. Now, if you'll excuse me, I'll let you three get…reacquainted. But don't wear yourselves out. There're plenty of engagements on the agenda. I'm confident you'll be able to find one that interests all three of you."

"We'll be sure to consider the options." Roman held up the envelope. "Thanks for dropping this off."

Glade tilted his head, taking one last perusal of the couple on the bed before heading out of the door. Roman closed it behind the man, turning in time to see Scarlet elbow Aiden hard in the chest, knocking him back before scrambling out from underneath him and stumbling off the bed. She snagged Roman's shirt off the chair where it had landed, tugging it on as she darted for the bathroom. Roman lunged after her, reaching the door as she slammed it behind her, the telltale click ringing through the room.

Aiden tripped in beside, him, trying to yank up jeans as he fell against the wall. He pulled them over his hips, not bothering to zip them up as he stared at the closed door, shaking his head. "What the fuck just happened?"

"Hell if I know. Scarlet?"

A muffled sob sounded from inside, the hollow noise like a knife to his chest.

He glanced at Aiden, noting the worry in the man's eyes. He leaned against the door. "Scarlet?"

"I can't do this." Another choked sob hiccupped through the door. "I'm sorry. I know I said I could...that there are lives at stake, but... I just can't be around you...knowing—"

He cursed, tossing the envelope on the bed before jimmying the lock then swinging open the door as he stepped through.

She turned, tears dotting her cheeks, the edges of her eyes slightly red. "Jesus Christ, Roman."

"No more locking us out."

"I wasn't... Go see what the hell Glade delivered. I need some time."

"Whatever's in that envelope can wait for five fucking minutes. We're going to deal with this, and we're doing it now."

"There's nothing to deal with, I'm just..."

He stalked toward her, stopping a foot away. "You're just what?"

She shook her head, pushing past him only to halt when Aiden barred the door.

"Not this time." Aiden backed her up. "We're working this out."

She turned, colliding with Roman. A throaty rasp feathered past her lips as he cornered her against Aiden, his lover's large body making hers look fragile.

"Look, I know we fucked up—*I* fucked up. That I let you down. Bolting the way I did—it was fucking cowardly. But I can't take back what I did. If I could..." Roman released a weary breath. "All I'm asking for is a chance to explain, even if the explanation doesn't justify my actions."

Scarlet frowned. "Do you honestly think this is just about you leaving? That I want to pull the plug on this case—put those women at risk—because I can't forgive you? Do you really think I'm that superficial?"

"Then what?" Roman traced his fingers along her jaw, brushing his thumb across the wet streaks on her cheek. "You always said you could tell me anything."

She closed her eyes for a moment, seemingly gathering her courage before staring up at him, determination firming her expression. "You want the truth? Fine. I can't stay here, having you both touch me, pretending that you're in love with me when I..."

"When you actually feel that way?" He leaned in, hovering his mouth next to hers. "You know, if you weren't so damn stubborn, you wouldn't be worrying about this."

"This isn't funny."

"I'm not saying it is." He took a few heavy steps away before turning. "Damn it, Scarlet, do you remember anything about that night?"

"I remember every detail in that studio intimately."

His cock peaked at her words. "You're not the only one. But I meant after—at the warehouse."

"I remember drawing down on those men. You getting clipped in the arm. Then Everett appeared behind you, his damn gun aimed at your head."

"And you pushed me out of the way."

"What the hell was I supposed to do? Let him kill you?" She shook her head. "Even I'm not that strong,

Roman. I did what a partner should do—what you would have done if our places had been reversed. And I won't apologize for it."

"Do you know what it was like to see you like that? God, you were so damn pale. I can still feel your blood on my skin, hear you struggling to breathe." He closed the distance between them. "You mumbled the entire time I carried you to the ambulance. Then just before they lifted you inside, you said something that changed everything. Do you remember?"

She pursed her lips, her chin quivering again.

He stroked her hair back from her face. "You told me you loved me."

She broke eye contact, toeing the floor before lifting her chin high. "You could have just told me you didn't feel the same. That you're in love with Aiden. Hell, I would have understood. You didn't have to leave—"

"Is that what you think? That I left because I *didn't* love you? Fuck, darling, I left because I *did*. Because I knew I couldn't go back to just being your friend, your partner. Making love to you in that damn studio might not have been the dream encounter I'd conjured in my fantasies, but that doesn't mean it wasn't every bit as real." He let his forehead rest against hers. "At the hospital... I didn't know what to think. I'd been in love with you for so fucking long..."

"But then why... I thought you and Aiden..."

He gave her a weak smile. "That was part of the problem. Aiden and I had been casual for a few months. Nothing I could ever fully commit to because..." He glanced at Aiden.

Aiden leaned in, lowering his mouth beside her ear. "Because he was in love with you. I knew that from the start. That you held a part of him no one else could. But the truly odd thing was...I never felt threatened. After Roman introduced us..." He chuckled. "You have a way of lighting up a room, of making anyone who's with you feel special. Didn't take me long to realize I was falling for you, too. Then you kissed me that night in the bar—"

"You remember that?"

"Couldn't forget it if I tried."

"Why didn't you ever say anything?"

"Same reason you didn't. Because it changed everything. At least, it did for me. I knew then that my heart belonged to both of you—I just didn't know how to broach the subject. So I waited. Then you were shot and Roman got scared. Not just of you but of everything. Everyone. Took him a month to stop running. By then..."

Roman sighed. "By then, I'd already been the biggest bastard I could be to you. So I tried to just let you go. But I can't...can't imagine my life without you and Aiden in it. I know we have to earn back your trust. Your love. All we're asking for is a chance. If you think there's any possibility you could find your way back to us..."

Her lips quirked. "And if this assignment hadn't popped up and thrown us all back together..."

"Then Aiden and I would be camped out on your front step for the week it would have taken before you let us in the damn door." He slid his lips softly across hers. "We'd made our decision when this bloody case got in our way. I'm done running. We both are. Let us prove it to you."

He moved slowly, just teasing her lips with his, waiting to see if his actions were welcomed. She held firm for a few moments before sighing out her breath, allowing her lips to mold to his. He stepped into the kiss, pressing her tight to Aiden's chest as he cupped the back of her head with one hand as the other glided down Aiden's side, landing on his hip. Aiden shifted slightly, allowing Roman to deepen the kiss before finally easing back, smiling at the woman nestled in their arms.

He nuzzled her nose, drinking in her warm, womanly scent. "Is that a yes?"

She stared up at him with those blue eyes of hers, innocence and sin warring with each other. She glanced over her shoulder at Aiden, giving him a tilt of her head. "Are you sure? I don't want to be a convenient third you tolerate because Roman—"

Aiden cut her off with the hard press of his mouth on hers, raising his hand to grip her hair. He gave the strands a tug, gaining him a soft moan mumbled around their kiss. Roman helped turn her into the Aiden's arms, sliding his hands down to her thighs where his shirt touched her skin. He massaged her flesh, slowly slipping his fingers under the material, humming as he smoothed them over her hips and up her ribs, stopping at the curve of her breasts. Her head fell into the crook of his shoulder when Aiden finally released her, his gaze dropping to where Roman's hands held the shirt, baring the rest of her.

"Fuck. You're beautiful." Aiden traced his finger up and down her ribcage. "Perhaps we should take Glade's advice and get...acquainted."

He backed up, extending his hand to her. She reached for him, easing out of Roman's embrace as she followed Aiden into the other room. The shirt fell to her thighs again—the material swaying seductively against her body. Roman trailed behind the couple, his heart hammering, chest heaving. Just thinking about finally loving her the way he'd pictured a thousand times made the room spin.

The mattress hit the backs of Aiden's legs, the crinkle of paper breaking the sensual atmosphere. He glanced down, cursing as the envelope Glade had given them scrunched slightly beneath him. He raised his gaze to Roman's, arching an eyebrow in question.

"Shit." Roman sighed, joining them at the bed. "Hold that thought, darling. We'll just see what our boss thought was important enough to chance having it delivered, regardless of his precautions."

He grabbed the sheets, tugging the pages off the outside before double-checking the security protocols. Convinced the contents hadn't been compromised, he thumbed open the end and glanced inside, frowning at the collection of items. He turned, flattening out a section of the blankets before dumping the materials on top. Graphic images glared at them, the photos openly mocking them.

Scarlet inhaled roughly, lifting one photo off the top. The bloody scene looked strangely surreal as she sank onto the mattress, the picture clenched between her fingers. "Oh, my God."

"Damn it!" Aiden grabbed a few more, shuffling through them. "This has to be the most violent kill yet."

"Kills." Roman held up a few more. "He murdered both sisters. In their vehicle, it appears." He grabbed the report, skimming through it. Rage burned hot in his gut as he read the damning details.

"What?" Scarlet gave him a shove. "I know that look on your face. What the fuck did he do this time?"

Roman looked at her, knowing the new developments wouldn't go over well. "It says that there's evidence of sexual assault with these two. Rather violent. Seems he used a knife after…"

Scarlet pushed to her feet, taking a few steps away from them before turning. She nodded, motioning to the photos. "Why change his MO?"

Roman shrugged. "He's taunting us. Showing us that he's smarter than we are. Profilers think he's evolving. Finding out what he likes, what brings him the release he seeks. Could be a number of reasons."

Aiden searched through the remaining pictures, picking up several. "Fuck! You two need to see these. Looks like he's started leaving pictures at the scene, too."

Roman moved in beside the man, allowing Scarlet to wedge between them. He stared at the images, ice sluicing through his veins. He'd kill the bastard. Simple as that. "That's...disturbing."

Scarlet scoffed. "Disturbing? Those are pictures of us. On the steps outside my house!" She snagged another one. "And this was taken inside the estate! It's of us kissing, for fuck's sake. That means he took this before he killed them, then he left them at the scene for the authorities to find." She stared up at them. "He's in the mansion. With us."

"Easy. Aiden and I won't let him touch you. Promise."

"You can't promise that. He could be anyone! One of Glade's staff, another guest. He obviously comes and goes as he pleases. And how the hell did he take these without anyone noticing?"

"The guy's a psychopath. You honestly think he's worried about smuggling a miniature digital camera in here? Besides, I've seen a couple of other guests with an illegal phone tucked in their pocket. We just didn't want to chance getting kicked out if Glade found out."

Aiden moved to her other side. "None of us are prisoners here. We can all leave. And we'll take you out if there's even a chance you're next. Our only saving grace is that he's killing the women in order — like it's part of his ritual. Chances are he can't deviate from the order because it's ingrained in his psychotic makeup." He held up his hands. "Not that either of us want more blood on our hands or more victims. We don't. But it does mean we have a bit of time before you pop up on his radar."

She stared at the photos, her shoulders drooping. "Are there pictures of all the other girls in here?"

Roman spread out the images, organizing them by model. "Oh, yeah. Here's one of Ms. October at a fucking gas station. Another of Ms. September grabbing donuts. It looks as if he followed more than one of us here. And I'll bet my ass these other images are from their residences, too."

Scarlet sighed. "This is crazy. He's more than a few steps ahead of us." She glanced at Aiden. "Can't the Feds use this as a means of forcing Glade's hands? Getting more agents inside?"

"There's no way to prove where these photos were taken, not the way they've been cropped." Aiden held up his palms. "Sure, we know the bastard's in here because we recognize when and where he took these. But to everyone else — there aren't any peripheral markers that can place us inside the manor. And the ones at your house don't help our current situation any. I just hope he doesn't know you're a cop."

"I don't wear a uniform or have a squad car. I guess he could have followed me to work but..."

"But we won't ever know for sure. Though he might have included a picture of that if he knew. A way of getting you kicked out of here so you don't jeopardize his other targets. Or just taunting you for fun. He obviously has a thing for power."

"So you're saying there's nothing the Bureau or the cops can do?"

"Not unless we're willing to break cover..."

"Damn it!" She stalked away, slapping the wall with her hand before spinning. "We can't do that. Not yet. If Glade kicks us out..." She leaned against the wall this time, allowing her head to fall against it. "If we come clean, can we get these girls in protective custody now?"

"Sure. But for how long?" Aiden looked between them. "I know neither of you want to hear this but...taking those women into custody isn't going to stop this guy. True, he might not kill them now, but what happens once this case goes cold? If he just sits and waits? We don't have the criteria to relocate them permanently. And who knows? Maybe it'll just antagonize the bastard...get him to start killing surrogates for these women." He shoved his hand through his hair. "I know this sounds harsh, but...our best chance at catching this creep is to stick to the plan. At least in here, he'll have to work to get to them."

"Right. And the fact there are so many people milling around at all hours can work to our advantage in this aspect. Harder for the guy to get any of the girls alone." She nodded. "So that's it. We stay until we catch him."

"We won't leave your side." Roman followed her across the room, laying one forearm above her head as he rested against her. "Won't give him an opportunity to get to you. Promise."

"Let's just finish this before Ms. July ends up like that."

"We'll do our best." He gave her a light kiss on the mouth. "We should look at the schedule. If this bastard is here, he'll be attending those damn games Glade has planned. No way a sexual predator like this guy is going to pass up watching people fuck. If we go to them, maybe we'll be able to narrow down the suspects. Observe a few men who look out of place or who display unsettling body language. If nothing else, keep an eye on the other girls. Our teams on the outside are combing through every bit of evidence. We'll figure this out."

"You boys do that. I'll get ready. Cover my scar while I decide which outfit will hide the most skin."

Roman cupped her waist, pulling her flush against him. "No one's going to touch you but us."

"Trust me, the gawking's bad enough." She gave his chest a pat as she headed for the bathroom. "Oh, and you boys still have some serious kissing up to do before you're truly forgiven. Don't think I've simply let you off the hook because you said some pretty words."

"Wouldn't expect anything less, darling." Roman winked at her. "But we meant what we said. We love you."

Aiden stepped beside Roman. "Both of us."

Her expression softened as she nodded, turning away before glancing at them over her shoulder. "I love you boys, too."

Roman smiled as the door closed partway, allowing them to see her reflection in the mirror. Damn, she was stunning. He nudged Aiden. "This ends. Quickly. I don't care what it takes, what risks *we* take. We solve this case and get the hell out."

"Nothing's going to happen to our girl. Case closed. Now come on. Let's see which events we think this guy will target before I decide it's not worth any risk and haul her ass out of here."

"Deal."

Roman moved over to the bed. So much for a tumble in the sheets to ease the tension. The case just got far more complicated. And if they didn't unearth a lead, the bastard would claim another life. And be one step closer to Scarlet.

Chapter Six

Scarlet palmed the counter in the bathroom, staring at her reflection in the mirror. "This can't be all of it, Roman. Please tell me there's a shawl, a hoodie. Anything."

She glanced to her left, staring at Roman as he leaned against the doorframe, hands stuffed into the pockets of his low-slung jeans. The red shirt he wore highlighted the deep brown tones in his hair and the slight bronze of his skin. Damn, he looked amazing.

He let his gaze travel the length of her body, the gleam in his eyes clearly showing his confusion. "You're fucking hot in that."

She stared back at the mirror. Wearing nothing but high heels, white velvet boy shorts that were more of a belt doing double duty and a matching bra, she resembled some kind of a fallen angel with a new faith — one that had absolutely nothing to do with saving the righteous.

"I look like a hooker."

"An incredibly beautiful one."

She scowled at him and he laughed.

"Darling. It's no worse than anything else you've worn. Okay, the shorts are pretty damn skimpy. Barely cover more than a thong but..." He gave her a stunning smile. "You certainly pull it off."

"This is payback, isn't it? For not talking to you boys that first day."

"Hey. If we had our way, we'd simply lock you in the room—keep you completely naked. But unfortunately, we can't catch a psychopath from in here. And there's no way you're going anywhere naked, other than our bed." He offered her his hand. "Come on. Glade has made it extremely clear that either we participate in one of his damn games today or he'll send us packing. Apparently, we're the only group who hasn't anted up, so to speak, in the three days we've been here."

"It's hard to think about sex when women are dying. Especially after learning those last two girls were lured out of here."

Scarlet rubbed her hands along her arms as a chill skittered down her spine, leaving a rash of goosebumps in its wake. It hadn't taken more than a few hours of poking around to learn that the two ladies had arrived before everyone else that first day and done a couple of photo sessions before returning to their room, after which they'd seemingly disappeared.

Scarlet had managed to sneak into their suite, but it was obvious they hadn't been killed there, let alone abducted. No signs of a struggle, with nothing out of place, it seemed reasonable that they'd most likely left on their own.

"Unfortunately, Thomas Glade doesn't share your aversion. If anything, the man's become even more invested in these games. I keep waiting for him to say something about those women who have seemingly just vanished, but he hasn't uttered a word."

"That's because the Feds got the police to release the original photos to placate the man. Stop him from canceling this entire retreat." Fuck, she was still fuming about that. Knowing her bare ass could be plastered all over his magazine and there wasn't a damn thing she could do until this case was over and she could slap an injunction in his lap.

Roman shook his outstretched hand, once again beckoning to her. She sighed, moving over to him, leaning into him as he wrapped her in his arms. God, he felt good. Right. Though they'd called a truce, there hadn't been a spare moment since they'd received the new pictures to do more than get a couple of hours sleep each night. Even then, they'd been switching off. Each man taking a turn slipping out to search for clues — spy on the other guests in the hopes of narrowing down their suspect list. Other than a few stolen kisses, the boys hadn't tried to seduce her. It was a fact that touched her heart more than they could know. Watching the blatant sex shows — part of her still worried it was the situation that had pushed them into action. But knowing they were willingly holding back — giving her a chance to work through the idea of being in love with two men at the same time — only made her love them more.

A click sounded behind her a moment before the door swung open and Aiden walked into the room. He gave them a smile, moving over to them then dipping his head down to taste her mouth. She pushed against him, silently demanding more. The man made a growling noise before tipping her head against Roman's chest as Aiden took control of the kiss, tasting every inch of her mouth before finally easing back.

He kept his face close, his blue eyes stealing her breath. "Damn, I've missed you."

"Right here."

He nodded, a sigh feathering across her cheek. "Not exactly the most romantic situation."

She traced her thumb along his stubbled jaw, enjoying the scratchy feeling. "Have I told you both how touched I am that you haven't pressured me? That you've made excuses at all those engagements and kept Glade off my back?"

"You've got a lot on your mind. We'll have plenty of time to keep you tied to our bed after this assignment's over."

She smiled. Damn the man was adorable when he talked dirty to her. "I agree tying me up under these circumstances might not be wise, but making love…"

The muscles in Aiden's jaw twitched. "Baby…"

Roman tapped her ass, gaining her attention. "You might want to hold onto those thoughts, because I'm not sure we can get out of some sort of public display today. We can't afford to make our benefactor suspicious. And the man's getting more impatient every day."

She snagged her bottom lip. "What choices do we have today?"

Roman snorted. "Fucking impossible to tell by the titles of the events. We'll just have to go and pray for the best." He leaned down and nipped at her neck. "Though I'm kind of hoping it involves licking you until you scream."

His words made her stomach flutter with anticipation. Fuck. Just thinking about it brought back memories of the studio. The way he'd made her come so hard she'd forgotten Everett was watching them.

Roman tsked her. "Are you thinking about the studio? You said you remembered every detail intimately. Do you remember what it felt like to have my tongue on your cleft? My fingers deep inside you?"

"God, Roman."

He smiled against her skin. "Soon, darling. But if we don't make an appearance, all this will be for nothing." He pulled back, his breath sending another wave of desire straight to her pussy. "Let's go. Just know this. Tonight, Aiden and I will do everything we can to seduce you into our bed...and for more than just sleeping."

She took a few shaky steps toward the door, using it to brace some of her weight, before glancing behind her. "All you have to do is say my name."

"Wench." Roman smacked her ass again as he joined her at the door. "I know you're aware of the drill but...stay close. If you sense anything out of the ordinary..."

She gave him a smile, noticing the way his eyes drifted up as he inhaled.

She leaned into him. "That scent is what you boys do to me."

He cursed behind her as she headed down the hall, laughing when they caught up to her. Aiden shook his head—the gleam in his eyes a dark promise. She hooked her arms through each of theirs as they made their way downstairs, heading for one of the parlors. Roman peeked into one, shaking his head at the row of handcuffs hanging at the opposite end. She gave him a raise of an eyebrow.

He snorted. "You want to be handcuffed... We have our own set. Multiple ones."

"So you're saying once we're home..."

"Fuck, darling. Keep teasing us like that and you *will* get a spanking."

She gazed up at him, unable to speak past the flood of desire that creamed her cleft. Aiden growled, tugged her against him as he claimed her mouth. She surrendered to the dominance in his touch, the way he smoothed his hands over her then squeezed her ass as he finally nipped his way down her neck. A couple pushed past them, muttering about them saving it for the show, before Aiden pulled away, keeping her possessively close.

He dropped a kiss on her nose. "Consider that particular fantasy first on the list. And in case you hadn't figured it out, we plan on having you live with us—whether it's at your place or ours. No more running."

Scarlet waited for uncertainty to scratch away the euphoric feeling warming her chest, but all she felt was peace. A sense of coming home.

"Deal. Now how about you guys find me a game I can handle."

Aiden's eyes widened, then he grinned. "Fuck, I love you. Roman. Our girl needs an event that won't make me want to kill any of the other guests."

"You and me both, buddy." Roman turned, her hand still gripped in his, when he nearly collided with Glade.

The man flashed them a knowing smile. "I'd have thought you three would be heading inside."

Roman moved closer to her, putting a protective arm around her. "While we applaud the use of restraints, it's not our mode of choice in a public forum."

Glade eyed them, openly sizing them up. "I respect your decision to keep your woman comfortable. Perhaps you'll find the activity in the ballroom more to your liking?"

"We'll head over there. Are you walking our way?"

"I am now."

The older man struck out ahead of them, his stride faster than she'd expected. Roman gave her hand a squeeze, walking behind the guy. Scarlet groaned inwardly. There'd be no chance of bowing out now, not with Thomas Glade accompanying them. Fucker would probably sit beside them, watching their every move.

Aiden's hand landed on the small of her back, his touch calming her. "Easy, baby. No matter what happens in that room, it's still us loving you. Nothing can change that, whether we're alone or surrounded by fifty people."

Warmth spread through her chest, tears misting her eyes. She looked at Aiden, wondering how she'd missed this side of him. Or had she chosen not to see it because she'd been scared? Either way, she wouldn't make the same mistake again. And she'd spend whatever time she had left showing both men how much their trust, their compassion meant to her. She mouthed her love, following Roman through the next set of doors. A variety of seating options encompassed most of the room, a raised stage lining the far wall.

Roman guided them over to a small love seat, tugging her onto his lap as Aiden scooted in beside them. He placed a hand on her thigh, the weight comforting. She rested against Roman, enjoying the play of muscles beneath her fingers. She hadn't gotten the chance to explore his body during their one encounter, and she longed to run her fingers over his taut frame, discover every dip and plane. Taste his skin, his release. Then she wanted to repeat every caress, every flick of her tongue, her lips on Aiden. Memorize their subtle differences. Learn what brought each man to his knees.

Roman brushed his lips across her ear. "If the look on your face is as telling as your scent, those thoughts running through your mind should be illegal."

"What you did to me in that studio should have been illegal."

The muscle in his jaw twitched. "Keep reminding me of that and I'll take you on this couch, crowd or not. And I know Aiden will help me."

She snagged her bottom lip. She'd never been with two men at once and she still wasn't sure what to expect—not emotionally.

Aiden leaned in. "You have to trust us, baby. I can see your uncertainty. But you know we'd never hurt you. Never rush you."

She jumped when a burst of static drowned out the murmur of voices. She twisted in Roman's lap, staring at the man standing on the stage as he tapped the microphone, smiling at the crowd.

He motioned to the chairs. "It's time for a little Christmas cheer, and what better present than a hot round of sex. There's just one catch—mouths only. Pick which one of you gives and which receives and give us your best shot. Oh, and remember. We'll need visual confirmation of completion. So fellas, we want to see that pussy cream and pulse."

Scarlet hissed out her breath. "Shit. There's got to be thirty people in here."

Her gaze landed on Glade, her stomach dropping at the knowing look in his eyes.

Roman sighed. "He's watching us. Waiting to see if we'll actually man up." He tilted his head, giving her an apologetic smile. "Don't think we can opt out of this one, darling."

Aiden pushed to his feet, extending his hand. "Nope. But it doesn't have to be you baring it all. The man did say we could choose who gave and who received. Unless you want me to stake my claim, because I really don't care how many people are in here. It'll just be us up there."

Her heart skipped, tripping back into a shaky rhythm as she accepted his hand, easing to her feet. "You'd do that? Be the one on display?"

He chuckled. "Do you have any idea how fucking hot your ass is in those shorts? Trust me. No one's going to be watching me. But if that helps you cope…"

He pulled her close, dropping a wet kiss on her before leading her to the stage. She glanced back at Roman, but he just smiled, crossing his legs as he leaned back, arms resting along the top of the couch.

Aiden stopped at the stairs, following her gaze. "Don't worry about Roman. Watching you suck me off is going to drive him wild. Promise. Now get your sexy ass up those steps before I decide it really should be your pussy beneath my tongue."

Scarlet released a shuddering breath. Fuck. The man could make her come from his words alone. She pressed against him, smoothing her hands up his chest as she nipped at his chin. "Guess it's a good thing I haven't eaten today."

She spun, putting extra swing in her hips as she climbed the steps to the stage, picking out a spot that afforded Roman the best view. She waited for Aiden to move in front of her before going to her knees, slowly clasping her hands behind her back. She bowed her head, giving him the semblance of submission as the rasp of his zipper echoed in her head. Other voices sounded around her, but she focused on the rustle of his jeans, the thud of them hitting the floor. She held her breath, praying she wouldn't lose her nerve when his hand grazed her face.

She looked up, humming out her breath. "God, damn, Aiden. You're spectacular."

His smile said everything she needed to know. "I'm not thrilled that this will be our…" He huffed. "I will have to spank you later. But for now, it's just us up here. And Roman's the only one watching."

"I love you."

His smile widened. She pushed the rest of the room out of her mind, concentrating on the hard lines of his muscles, the way his broad shoulders narrowed into his lean waist, taut bands across his abdomen creating shadows on his skin. The man was grace and strength rolled into a breath-taking package, and he was hers.

She leaned forward, inhaling his masculine scent. Spicy man mixed with cocoanut soap teased her senses and she nuzzled his groin, loving that he kept himself bare. That she'd be able to lick every inch of his shaft and the heavy sac that hung between his legs. She traced her lips along his length, giving him just a hint of her tongue as she stopped level with the head, smiling at the bead of fluid gracing the tip.

She looked up at him, eyebrows raised. "Horny, baby?"

He speared his fingers through her hair, holding the mass back from her face. "Since I met you." He tightened his grip. "No teasing."

"Don't you want me to put on a show?"

"Next time." He growled at her smug grin. "Scarlet."

The deep rumble in his voice made her stomach flutter, the unspoken command peaking her nipples against her bra. Now, he had her thinking about both men spanking her, and fuck, if it didn't make her wet. A hot swirl of need coiled in her groin.

Aiden tugged on the strands bunched in his hand, drawing her attention. "Are you picturing me spanking you? Or are you picturing both of us?" He released a raspy breath. "Shit, baby. I can't wait until we get you home. You're going to be so damn busy for the next fifty years. But for now..."

Scarlet dipped forward to drop a kiss on the end of his cock. It jerked in response, bobbing up toward his abdomen before settling in front of her face again. She wanted to wrap her fingers around his thick length — feel the contrast between silky skin and rock-hard strength. Scratch a line to the crown with her nails, knowing the sensation drove him mad.

Instead, she poked out her tongue, moving slowly, wanting Aiden to anticipate the first flick across his flesh. His stomach clenched at the gentle contact, once again raising his cock. She waited as it descended, this time angling her head above the crown. He moaned as she lapped at his skin, licking the slippery fluid away. She hummed at the unique flavor of him, making a second pass. Salty spice bathed her tongue, making more juice cream her cleft. Damn, she didn't just want to suck him off, she wanted to fuck him. And Roman. Feel them surrender themselves to her — give herself to them in every way.

She pushed aside her desires. There'd be time to delve into them later. For now, she soothed the ache tingling her clit by focusing on Aiden. The smooth glide of his shaft against her mouth, the twitch of his muscles as she spread her lips, taking him deep inside.

"Fuck, baby. So damn hot and wet." He hissed out his next few breaths, clenching his fingers in her hair. "Like Heaven and Hell."

She hollowed her cheeks as she slowly retreated, pressing her tongue against the thick veins lining the underside. She kept the crown encased within her mouth, sucking on the head, before sinking down again, taking him as far as she could to the back of her throat.

His breathing increased, soft murmurs of encouragement sounding around her. She pulled free this time, dipping beneath his shaft to nuzzle his sac. She took her time, laving his skin before mouthing each side. His body tensed, a distinctive grunt spurring her on.

Aiden tugged on her hair, guiding her back to his cock, pressing the tip against her mouth. "Take me deep, Scarlet. And don't stop this time. I'm too fucking close."

He began moving with her, sliding his cock deep inside her mouth then easing it back, never quite halting his movements. He thrust his hips back and forth, the steady rhythm obviously building his need. She glanced up at him, hands still clasped behind her back, pumping his shaft into her mouth. He met her gaze, gritting his teeth as he tilted his head back, the muscles in his neck cording from the tension. She opened wider, allowing him to set the pace, knowing his loss of control would be her reward.

He tried to meter his thrusts, hips jerking as he obviously fought against the rush of pleasure that flushed his skin. She could track the progression of it. How his sac pulled tight to his body, his cock weeping additional precious fluid along her tongue. He fisted his fingers then released them, the sporadic twitches tingling her clit until she feared she might climax from just the feel of his hands in her hair.

"Damn. Scarlet. I can't hold off. You're so fucking hot. So much pressure." He hung his head in seeming defeat. "Shit, they want to see me..."

She growled her defiance, sealing her mouth more forcefully around him. His gaze snapped to hers before his eyes squeezed shut, a muffled curse rasping free. He tried to pull her head back, but she refused. He could shoot the last of his release on her chest. But she wouldn't surrender without a taste. Without knowing she'd won.

"Fuck. Scarlet."

His words sounded harsh. An echoed groan rose from the crowd. Aiden pumped into her mouth a dozen more times before his body stiffened, the first pulse of his seed coating her tongue. She hummed her victory, swallowing two more shots before reaching for his cock, angling the head at her chest. He came again, this spurt splashing across her breasts, the warm feel of his release making her pussy clench emptily. She didn't want him to finish on her skin. She wanted to taste every drop. Have Roman pound into her from behind. Vanquish the burning need deep inside her.

Aiden emptied three more pulses onto her flesh, finally bowing over her, chest heaving as his hold in her hair finally loosened. It took what felt like several tries before his hands fell from her head, and he went to his knees in front of her. He cupped her jaw as he raised her face to his, his mouth crushing down possessively over hers. She allowed him complete control, hoping her surrender would ease the tension in his muscles as they flexed beneath her hands. Aiden sighed once they'd finally parted, forehead resting on hers, their breath mixing. He gave her one last gentle kiss, stealing her heart more with the soft press of his lips than when he'd conquered her.

He thumbed the corner of her mouth. "I love you. You know that, right?"

She gave him a genuine smile. "I think you destroyed any doubts when you stepped up on that stage. Do you know what that meant to me? Having you as the focus, the one bared?"

"Like I said. I don't compare to you, baby. They hardly saw me beyond that ass of yours. But if it made you feel better…"

"That's not why you did it and we both know it." She kissed him again. "Thank you."

He nodded, glancing at her chest. "Shit. I owe you a bath."

"If I'd had my way, there wouldn't be a mess to clean up."

"Naughty wench. You always did rebel against the rules."

He eased back, helping her to her feet before yanking up his pants. The guy with the microphone sauntered over, drawing his finger through the remnants of Aiden's climax still clinging to her skin as he gave them a creepy smile.

He turned to the crowd. "Seems our Christmas angel knows how to give head. A round of applause for Ms. December."

Scarlet plastered on a fake smile, picking her way back to Roman, ignoring the blatant leers from the men sitting in the crowd. Aiden kept his hand on the small of her back, the constant pressure grounding her. She stopped at the love seat, attention focused on Roman as he shifted his gaze to her chest, the muscle in his jaw twitching. He stood, holding up a wet towel one of Glade's staff must have given him, before brushing it across her skin, removing the last bits of sticky fluid.

Aiden moved in close. "Anyone stand out?"

"Yeah. Everyone. They're all strange in some way. I did notice that Glade has his photographer taking candid shots. Not sure it's that simple, but..." He shrugged. "He's definitely on the short list. He's the one person who can openly film the guests without question. And we should try to get a look at his darkroom. Maybe while he's busy during one of the photo sessions. I also saw Ms. November scowling throughout the entire show. Her partner nudged her, but she flipped him off, choosing to watch."

"Not everyone wants to be on stage. Maybe they had a fight?"

Roman nodded, looking up when Glade stepped over to them. He greeted the older man. "Well?"

Glade grinned, the look on his face slightly unnerving as he finally focused on Roman again. "It would appear your partners know how to put on a show. I haven't seen a man come that hard in years. She has quite the wicked mouth."

Roman wrapped his arm around her. "That she does."

Glade motioned to Aiden. "Perhaps you two gentlemen will give us an equally good display later? Based on that kiss that first night, I assume you two are lovers, as well."

"Of course. We just figured the purpose of the gathering was to showcase our girl." Roman ran his fingers through the ends of her hair. "After all, it's her ass everyone wants to see."

"Not just her ass." He took a step back. "Lovely seeing the three of you again. Enjoy the rest of your day."

He wandered off, whistling to himself.

Roman frowned, shaking his head before turning back to them. His gaze fell to the cloth, his vein pulsing again. He grabbed Scarlet by the waist, tugging her tight against him as he smoothed one hand over her buttocks, squeezing her flesh. "You'd best get your ass back to our room before I fucking mount you right here, because, darling, I'm one breath away from completely losing control." He nodded at Aiden. "You, too, or we really will give these folks a show."

Roman wove his fingers through hers and headed out with Aiden bringing up the rear. The man's hand never left the small of her back, and she had a hunch that both men were feeling more than a little possessive right now. And if their pace was any indication, she was in for one hell of a ride.

Chapter Seven

Roman tugged Scarlet behind him, every thought centered on reaching their room and finally loving her the way he'd been envisioning for the past three months. Hell, the past two years. Only this time, it wouldn't be a fantasy. It wouldn't end with his hand around his dick, calling her name to nothing but the splash of the water against the shower wall. And he wouldn't be alone.

The steady footfalls of Aiden behind him only increased the need hammering at Roman's head. They'd never shared a woman—never wanted another to join them—other than Scarlet. And he knew his buddy was just as invested as he was. Roman could tell by the way Aiden had looked at him from the stage, the man's cum still smeared on Scarlet's chest. Aiden wasn't the sort of guy to embrace public displays, but he'd pushed aside his own feelings to spare Scarlet hers. And Roman loved the man more for that simple sacrifice.

He stopped at their room, opening the door with a twist of the key in the lock. Roman liked the nostalgic feel of a key—the comforting weight of it in his pocket—and was glad Glade hadn't opted to modernize his old mansion in that particular fashion. It also meant picking locks was a viable option if needed.

The old door creaked open, swinging against the wall as Roman marched inside and turned once he'd cleared the doorway. A throaty moan was all the warning he gave Scarlet before backing her into Aiden's chest. Her breath left her on a hiss as he pressed his body against hers, leaving just enough room for Aiden's hands to cup her waist. A low hum accompanied Roman's touch as he smoothed his fingers up her ribcage, stopping just below her breasts.

She forced in a quick breath, her heart beating a tattoo beneath his hands. "Roman—"

He cut her off with a single finger pressed to her lips. He moved impossibly closer, brushing his chest across her nipples. Her head fell back against Aiden's shoulder as the light motion tightened the tiny buds further, pushing them out against the thin material. Roman smiled, flicking his thumb over one turgid peak as he lowered his lips to her neck.

"There's not a doubt in my mind that you want this. Need it as much as we do. But I promised not to rush you, and if you're not ready to move beyond what we've already shared—if you need more time before we take you into our bed—I'll respect that, but…"

He sighed, feathering his breath across her skin. She arched into him, clenching her jaw as he scraped his teeth along the hollow of her shoulder.

He ended it with a light bite before meeting her gaze again. "I need you. We both do. So damn much it hurts."

She kissed the finger still pressed to her lips, tracing the line of his jaw before tunneling her hands through his hair. She guided his head closer to hers, nipping at his bottom lip. "I need you and Aiden, too. Now I believe you mentioned something about losing control."

"Dangerous challenge, darling, especially when you know how close to the edge we are." He dropped a soft kiss behind her ear, smiling at her whispered gasp. "But if you truly trust us, we'll show you how we've been dreaming of loving you all this time."

He nodded at Aiden, smiling when the man lifted his hand, cupping one breast and holding it out to Roman.

He held her gaze as he dipped down, laving her nipple through her skimpy top before using his teeth and holding the nub captive. He bit down just enough to make her moan, before releasing and raising his face level with hers. He brushed his lips across hers, tasting her anticipation. The scent of her desire wafted around them, stronger than when they'd left their room earlier, and he couldn't wait for her reply. Her mouth was too close, her lips too damn full to wait. He slanted over her, testing their softness, forcing himself to go slowly. If this was going to work — be something more permanent than a few days away from the rest of the world — he and Aiden needed to seduce her into their bed. Lure her with tempting touches and fleeting caresses designed to leave her wanting more. Though he knew she was committed to them, actually making love to both of them was a huge step. No matter how much she wanted it.

She hesitated, her lips touching his, her breath a sweet bounty of chocolate and spice. He hedged his bet, tracing her bottom lip with his tongue, dipping just the tip inside her mouth. A breathy little whimper was the only indication he'd won before her hands curled around his neck, raking through his hair.

Roman moaned his victory, plunging his tongue inside her wet heat, using Aiden's shoulder to tilt her back and deepen the kiss. His lover growled, shifting his hands to cover her breasts, finding just the right amount of pressure with his fingers to make her groan into Roman's mouth. Roman pulled back, watching her eyelids flutter open, her lips still parted, the edges wet and swollen. She moaned again when Aiden tweaked her nipples harder.

Roman gazed down at her. "So is that an unequivocal yes?"

Scarlet tilted her head back to look at Aiden. He dipped down, brushing his lips across hers, tracing their fullness with his tongue. He eased away when she tried to kiss him, his smile causing the breath to hiss from her chest.

Aiden quirked an eyebrow. "We need to know you're ready. This is more than a tumble in the sheets. I've already told you. Roman and I want you in our lives—permanently. If you have even the slightest doubt that now is the time to take this next step…"

"I'm more than ready. But I won't lie. I've never…" She sighed. "I'm just a bit nervous what you…what you both expect of me. Once we're all in the heat of things, and…" A deep flush laced down her chest. "I don't want to disappoint you. What if I don't live up to your fantasies?"

"No fucking way. Just holding you like this, having you sleep beside us, is better than anything we've conjured up in our dreams."

A slow smile spread across her face. "Then stop questioning me and make love to me." She shook her finger when Roman rimmed her shorts. "Not so fast, *lover*. I want a chance to taste you first, Roman. Aiden just allowed me that pleasure — however unconventional it was — and as I recall, you denied me three months ago. I won't be denied again." She smoothed her hands along his shoulders, smiling at the twitch of his muscles. "Do we have a deal?"

Scarlet's heart thrummed as Roman narrowed his eyes, his breath a rough caress across her neck. He hesitated for a few, agonizing heartbeats, then smiled, slowly easing away. He raised his hands, palms up, allowing her to switch their positions, pushing him against the wall as she moved in front, Aiden shadowing her every move. She swept her gaze down the length of his body, determined to discover every inch of him. Though they'd made love in that damn studio, she'd yet to knead his muscles with her fingers. Feel his skin glide beneath hers. He'd claimed her, and she needed to do the same in return.

Scarlet released her breath, shifting her gaze to Aiden, flashing him an inviting smile before sliding her hands down to Roman's waist. The sharp hiss of metal echoed her moan as she lowered his zipper, freeing his erection. He looked even larger than she remembered, and both men groaned as she traced a single finger along his length, making the head flare beneath her gentle touch.

"Pants, baby. Now." She turned to Aiden, watching his eyes flicker between Roman's shaft and her. "You, too. Or were you just going to watch this round? Admire from afar as Roman did in the parlor?"

"No fucking way." He fisted the rough material, tearing the seam in his rush to strip them off.

Scarlet purred. The men were alike in so many ways. Both had thick rippling muscles, tight little asses and cocks that would make any woman drool. She smiled as they tossed their clothes to the ground, bracketing her between them. Aiden released the clasps of her top, letting it fall as Roman pushed her shorts over the curve of her ass, dropping the material at her feet. A chorus of moans had her clenching her thighs, hoping to keep her juice from dripping on the floor.

Aiden eased forward skimming his lips down the curve of her neck. "That's how Roman wants you, baby. Naked. Wet. So hot for his cock you can't see straight. Now kneel in front of him but make sure you keep those sexy legs nice and wide. He'll want to see what he does to you...what we both do to you. I didn't get the luxury of having you do that on stage. Didn't want you to reveal more of your sexy body so those other men could see what's ours. And you *are* ours. Make no mistake. From this moment forward, you belong to us as much as we do to you."

Scarlet tiptoed up, kissing the rough stubble on Aiden's chin." Wouldn't want it any other way. I'm done running from you boys. Now stop talking and put that mouth to good use."

"Fuck!"

Aiden crushed his mouth on hers, the kiss hard. Demanding. He didn't stop until she surrendered complete control to him, her chest heaving frantically by the time he finally eased back. He gave her ass a light tap before turning her to back to face Roman. Aiden cupped her waist as he lowered them both to the floor, settling her between his thighs. Roman's dick arched proudly toward her face, the tip glistening with evidence of his arousal. She leaned forward, breathing in his heady scent. Although slightly different than Aiden's, it reminded her of fire and spice and she didn't wait for his invitation. She distended her tongue, bathing the head with long, slow pulls, humming at the exquisite taste of him.

Roman grunted, tracing one finger along her cheek. "Goddamn, Scarlet. You keep licking me like that and I won't last a minute."

She smiled up at him, taking just the head inside her wet heat before pulling back and nipping at the plump crown. "That works for me. Maybe Aiden would like a repeat performance?"

Aiden chuckled against her neck, tweaking one nipple. "Wench. What I need is to fuck you. But we'll get there in time. For now, concentrate on Roman. Imagine how he felt watching you lick me. Taking me deep to the back of your throat, knowing every other man in the room wanted to be me. To be close enough they could smell your desire, just as we can now. And you smell delicious."

Aiden's words made her pussy clench, the empty sensation fluttering need through her core. She used Roman to stem that feeling, sinking half his length inside her mouth. Roman grunted, threading his fingers through her hair, tugging on the long strands just enough to cause a slight sting. She moaned around his cock as Aiden smoothed his hands down her torso, letting them settle on her thighs.

"Open wider, baby. We can't see that beautiful pussy near enough."

She did as he asked, spreading her knees farther apart, giving them a clear view of her sex, and her arousal. It slid along her inner lips, a small amount easing down one thigh. Roman cursed and tightened his hold as Aiden nipped at the side of her neck.

"Nice." Aiden, trailed his hand up her groin, gathering some of her cream on his fingers. He smiled as he brought them to his mouth, sucking off her juice.

Scarlet released Roman's cock, dragging Aiden to her with a curl of her fingers. He took her challenge, thrusting his tongue into her mouth, claiming her as Roman had their first time. She matched his hunger, shadowing his mouth until her lungs burned, and she pulled back.

"He tastes good on you. But I knew he would." Aiden smiled, nodding at the juice trailing down her thighs. 'Soon,' he mouthed, motioning back to his lover's shaft.

She licked her lips, devouring Roman's cock, swallowing his thick length in one determined motion. He was slightly bigger than Aiden, the large width barely fitting inside her mouth. She relaxed her muscles, working him deeper, knowing the pressure would increase his need.

His abdominal muscles clenched, outlining the bands cording beneath his flesh. "Yeah, darling. Just like that."

His voice echoed in her head, his fingers still caressing her scalp. Aiden shifted closer, teasing the edge of her sex, dipping just the tip of his finger inside her. She closed her eyes, loving the feel of Roman's cock sliding along her tongue as Aiden caressed her body, spreading traces of her juice across her nipples and stomach, as if he intended to lick it clean later.

Aiden leaned in beside her, kissing the side of her mouth. She paused when his tongue caressed her lips, flicking over Roman's cock as she moved up and down his length. She eased Roman's shaft free as she pressed back on her heels, holding his cock out to Aiden, arching her eyebrow in challenge. Aiden accepted, shifting forward, sampling his lover's crown with such feral intent she had to stop herself from coming on the spot. The act was erotic and hot and she loved watching the men interact.

Scarlet twisted slightly, wrapping her hand around the length Aiden couldn't reach then pumping the hard shaft in time with the Aiden's bobbing motion. The man was masterful, applying a suction she doubted she could've given. She watched him work Roman's length then leaned in, tracing Aiden's lips with her tongue before trailing it down Roman's shaft, dropping beneath him to suckle his sac. She reveled in their unified groans as she retraced her steps, once again licking at Aiden's lips.

Aiden pulled free, his hand pumping with hers as he filled her mouth with his tongue, the heady essence of Roman's pre-cum mixing with the distinct taste that was all Aiden. She moaned at the combined flavors, turning back to Roman when the man groaned, his thighs tensing.

Scarlet pushed Aiden back, reclaiming Roman's cock for herself. If he was going to fill someone's mouth, it was sure as hell going to be hers.

Aiden chuckled, roaming his hands across her body as she quickened her pace, edging Roman even closer. Roman cursed, thrusting his hips, taking her mouth in long steady strides. His lips pursed tight as he tilted his head back. She sucked harder, massaging his sac, locking him deep in her throat when his cock shuddered, then flared, his movements faltering.

"He's going to come, Scarlet. Swallow all of it."

Her clit pulsed at Aiden's command, her pussy clamping around the ghosted penetration of the man's finger. She moved faster, taking Roman even deeper as he pounded into her three more times before filling her mouth with the spicy fluid of his release. Her name slipped from his lips as he jerked against her, his body purging every drop. She looked up, his cock still trapped inside her mouth until Aiden pulled her back, leaving Roman's shaft to fall free.

She moved with him, easing her body against his, loving the feel of his skin on hers. He dragged kisses along her shoulder and she tilted her head, giving him better access as her eyes drifted closed. A low moan floated around them as he clenched her muscle between his teeth, leaving his mark, his ownership. She fluttered open her eyelids as Roman kneeled in front of her, framing her face with his hands.

"And you were worried you wouldn't measure up? Fuck, darling, you damn near killed me."

She welcomed his open-mouthed kiss, knowing he'd taste his own release on her tongue as Aiden discovered every dip and curve of her body with his hands. Roman swallowed her cry when Aiden danced his fingers across her mound, teasing her clit this time.

Hard pants racked her chest as Roman pulled back, his gaze settling on her pussy. Aiden parted her drenched lips, revealing her small nub to the cool air. A hiss sounded in her head when her body clenched at the sudden chill, making her clit flutter.

"Damn, I love it when you do that." Roman lowered between her spread thighs, swiping his tongue through her slick crease.

She threw her head back against Aiden's shoulder, unable to keep the fire at bay. She twisted in her fingers in the thick strands of Roman's hair as she anchored him to her, pushing her pussy hard against his mouth.

He chuckled once, lapping at her sex, nipping her lips until she was certain she'd explode. She tilted her hips, needing him to increase the pressure, but he pulled back, meeting her gaze, his mouth covered in her juice.

"Sorry, but I already got to taste your sweet release. And I promised Aiden he'd get his chance."

He laughed as his lover scooped her up and carried her to the bed. God, it felt so right in Aiden's arms, the way she'd felt in Roman's, and she knew she'd come home. She whispered Aiden's name as he draped her across the bed, waiting for Roman to position himself before shuffling her against him. Roman groaned and hooked her knee, lifting one thigh over his as Aiden settled between her legs, curling the other around Aiden's shoulder. Aiden drew a deep breath, licking his lips at the sweet scent mixing around them.

Roman reached over her, using his fingers to open her to Aiden's gaze. "Now be a good girl, and show Aiden just how delicious you are."

Scarlet held her breath, anticipating that first touch when Aiden lapped at Roman's fingers, tracing where they held her flesh before licking a path through her cleft.

Her breath left her on a hiss, his tongue hot against her skin. "Oh God, Aiden."

She arched back, her hair fanning across Roman's shoulder as Aiden worked two fingers inside her, moaning at the tight clasp of her pussy.

"Fuck, Roman. She's so tight." He pushed again, making her body convulse around him. "Oh, Scarlet. I can't wait to feel you do that to my cock."

Scarlet fought the rush of pleasure, wanting to come, but not wanting the surreal moment to end. She still couldn't believe she was sandwiched between them, praying they'd take her before she melted in their arms. She arched upwards, seeking release, but stilled at the feel of Aiden's finger against her ass.

"So beautiful, baby. Damn, you have the most magnificent ass." He probed again, inching inside.

She blinked in surprise, shifting her gaze to Roman.

"Easy. Aiden only wants to touch you." He dropped a wet kiss on her open lips. "Have you ever had a man fuck you there before?"

She snagged her lip between her teeth, shaking her head as Aiden's finger sank deeper, igniting a fire inside her hot channel.

"Then we'll be honored to be your first." He nipped at her lip this time. "Relax, Scarlet. Trust us. We won't ask to take you like that until you're ready."

She nodded and closed her eyes, unsure if the sensation was pleasing, until Aiden locked his finger inside her as he engulfed her clit in his mouth. A sound, primal and raw, broke free from her lips as spikes of pleasure rippled through her, starting in her ass and ending in her sex. The feeling was nothing she'd experienced before, and she cried out, as her release loomed closer, arching her hips off the bed.

Aiden hummed, sucking her clit, pumping his finger back and forth through her ass, spiraling her higher. Roman nipped at her ear, sliding one hand through her slit, sinking two fingers into her sex. The dual penetration sent her over, snapping the coil strung tight in her belly and unleashing waves of heat so fierce she expected her skin to singe. Both their names sounded through the room as she twisted on the bed, consumed by the sheer magnitude of her climax. Colored dots flashed at the edges of her vision as her body slowly descended, her limbs going limp at her sides.

"God, I love watching you come." Roman bent over her, teasing her lips with just the hint of a kiss. "Let's do it again."

Aiden and Roman lifted her up, shifting her around until she was resting on her hands and knees. Roman moved in behind her, skimming his fingers along her ass, tracing the valley between her cheeks as he grazed his finger across her anus. She moaned, watching Aiden recline in front, holding his arms out to her. She glanced down his body. His cock was hard and thick, stretching out achingly toward her.

She shuffled over to him, straddling his thighs as his hands landed on her hips. He guided her lower, nudging his shaft against her sex, pausing to see if she'd grant him access. She snagged her bottom lip, rotating her hips before lowering her weight, taking him deep inside her.

Aiden pressed his head into the mattress, clenching his fingers around her flesh. "Ah, fuck, Scarlet. Damn, your pussy is hot."

She purred as she eased up, dragging his cock through her channel, stopping with the head still clenched within her. She hovered above him, savoring the anticipation of her next pass before descending again, allowing her head to tip back as his shaft stretched her. Fire spread through her sex, coiling another orgasm in her groin.

Roman landed a smack on one side of her ass, his lips feather soft against her ear as he covered her with his body. "Are you teasing him? Naughty little wench. And you'll pay for allowing me to take you from behind again, even if that first time was a concession. Because I will claim you once Aiden makes you scream. And when it's time, Aiden will help me spank you."

She moaned, picturing the scene. Both men sitting opposite each other, their legs entwined, her body curled over them. Her ass would be raised, ripe for their choosing, as they took turns caressing her pale skin. She could sense their carnal intent, feel their lingering promise as they each raised a hand, connecting with her flesh in turn, raining down her punishment until she begged for mercy. Then they'd pleasure her, fingers pumping through her ass and pussy, each feeling the other's penetration until her body surrendered, locking them both in place.

Roman tsked her. "You're imagining it, aren't you?"

She could only nod, his finger circling her ass as she rode Aiden, white-hot need burning through her veins.

Roman's breath washed over her shoulder, the feathery sensation sending goosebumps along her skin. "Good, 'cause you're ours to pleasure. Ours to protect. Make no mistake about that. And if you endanger what's ours, you'll be treated accordingly."

Scarlet locked Aiden deep inside her, pausing just long enough to glance back at Roman over her shoulder. "As long as I get the same concessions. You boys risk what's mine and you'll be the ones tied to the bed."

Roman's eyes darkened at her words. "Deal. Now finish him. He's been more than patient."

She cried out as Roman helped lift her up, holding her tight as Aiden pounded into her from below, fucking her like a man possessed. She clenched her fingers around Aiden's shoulders, knowing she was probably leaving tiny, crescent-shaped marks on his skin but too far gone to care. Her impending orgasm licked at her senses, dimming her vision until nothing remained by the feel of Aiden thrusting inside her and

Roman's hands around her waist. She held her breath, her body clenching tightly when a finger landed on her clit.

She broke, shouting out her release as Aiden stiffened below her, hissing her name as his cock pulsed, coating her walls with his essence. Pleasure spiraled outwards from her core, a comforting heat finally bringing her back down.

Aiden levered up, circling his arms around her as he dropped kisses along her neck. "God, baby. I've never..." His breath washed over her skin. "You're incredible."

She gave him a weak smile, not sure she had the strength to do more than huddle in his arms when he relaxed back, taking her with him. Her hips tilted upwards, allowing Aiden's cock to slip free as Roman smoothed his hands across her flesh, the dark promise of his touch reawakening her senses. She moaned as he probed her tight pucker before trailing his finger through her folds.

"Fuck. Watching you come around Aiden... Best damn show I've ever seen. But next time, I won't wait to claim you — I'll be deep inside your sweet ass for the first time. You want that, don't you? Want us both filling you?"

"God, yes."

"Next time. For now, close your eyes and scream for me."

Roman placed his shaft at her sex, plunging home in one swift motion. The hard penetration sent her soaring again, the sensations too strong to deny. She clawed at Aiden's chest, chanting Roman's name as he pistoned into her, every stroke harder than the last, sending him deeper inside her until his possession consumed her every thought. His hand connected with her buttocks, the sharp sting fluttering her clit.

"Now, please. God, so good."

His hand landed a second time.

"Yes. Again, Roman. I need…"

Her voice keened into a wail as he rained down four more slaps, each one pulsing her clit until her body exploded, a rush of warm cream coating his thrusting cock.

"Fuck, yeah, Scarlet. Keep coming."

Aiden joined in, tweaking her nipples then pinching her clit, keeping her suspended until the room faded and she collapsed on Aiden, her entire body convulsing.

"Gonna come. So damn hot."

Roman claimed her three more times before he shouted her name, grinding his pelvis against her ass as he climaxed inside her, every jerk of his hips pushing her further under. Voices swirled in the background, but all she could make out was the steady thrash of Aiden's heart beneath her ear.

Roman leaned over her, dropping kisses on her shoulders and back as he eased free. She whimpered at the loss, but he shushed her, drawing her hair back from her face.

"Easy, darling. Rest."

The men shuffled her around until she was positioned between them, their constant caresses soothing her heated skin, lulling her into a light sleep. She wanted to tell them she loved them, but nothing more than a rasp made it past her lips as she drifted off, their promise of more following her into the darkness.

Chapter Eight

"I swear to God I'll kill that man!"

Scarlet stomped into the room, rubbing her arms as she shivered amidst the layers of clothing, wondering if she'd ever be warm again.

Roman moved in behind her, tugging her against his chest as he curled his arms around her. "Now, now, darling. We can't go around killing everyone who pisses you off. We'd never have time for anything else."

"Very funny." She elbowed him and was rewarded with a muted grunt. "And I'll be satisfied with just him."

Aiden stepped in front of her, pressing his chest against hers as he helped rub her arms. "Nick is only following Glade's instructions. You're Ms. December. He wants photos of you out in the snow."

"It's not being out in the snow that bothers me. It's having to do it dressed in a freaking red bustier and a thong!"

"The photographer did allow you a nice set of velvet boots and hat."

"And don't forget that muff." Roman gave her a squeeze. "Oh the things we could do to you with that soft piece of fur."

"Fuck off. Both of you." She tried to tug out of their embrace, sighing when she did little more than rub her hard nipples against Aiden's chest. *Fuck.* They were still sore from being puckered for over an hour, and she wasn't sure she could take any additional stimulation.

Aiden tsked her. "I'm guessing you don't have much of a sense of humor right now. Fine. You cuddle with Roman, and I'll run you a bath. Quickest way to get warm."

She huffed, though she could tell by the way Aiden flashed her a sloppy grin he knew it was just for show. Roman shifted his hands, scooping her up and carrying her to the bed. He placed her gently on top then methodically removed her clothes. Shivers raked through her, and she was certain her skin had a blue tinge to it.

"Damn. You look like a fucking Smurf." He grabbed a soft fleece blanket off the end of the bed and wrapped her in it. "And you won't have to kill Nick. I swear if that camera boy adjusts your breasts one more time, I'll shove that lens up his ass." He pulled her back onto his lap after sitting on the edge. "It's bullshit that you weren't showing enough cleavage. I could see your nipples from across the fucking lawn." He hissed out a breath, fluttering her hair around her face. "I know all the checks we've done on him and the other staff have some back clean, but...something feels off about him. It's as if he's over attentive one minute then acting as if he can't stand to touch you the next. And Ms. November wasn't much better."

"Candi?"

"She's nothing like candy, darling."

Scarlet laughed. "No, I think her name is Candi. At least, that's what it sounded like when Nick called her over. She's quite secretive, though I can't blame her. If I'd been smart, I would have picked a different first name."

"Hey. We all know the first rule of being undercover is to stick as close to the truth as possible. And thankfully here, they don't want to know more than a first name for the ladies. Even that is optional."

Scarlet leaned into him, exhaustion straining her muscles. "So what didn't you like about Ms. November? And didn't you mention her before?"

"Yeah. She scowled the other day during your public display."

Her cheeks heated at the memory, though just as much from what had happened once they'd returned to the room as from having to give Aiden a blow job in front of a crowd.

He chuckled. "I know you're remembering what you did to Aiden. Poor man never stood a chance. As for Candi—or whatever her name is—it's not anything I can pinpoint. More of a feeling. The way she watches you when you're not looking her way. I don't think she likes the competition up here."

"Sorry to burst your bubble, baby, but most of these women are far savvier than me when it comes to being a cover model. I keep expecting Glade to come to his senses and kick me out."

"Are you staring at the same body in the mirror as we are? Because, damn, you're gorgeous."

She grinned, leaning over to kiss his stubbled jaw. "Thanks. You boys are pretty damn hot yourselves. Unfortunately, being hot isn't helping us in this instance." She sighed. "At least Glade's added security measures seem to be working. All the other models are still present and accounted for. Having them travel with a companion has definitely hampered this guy."

"Which only makes him more dangerous. He's going to get desperate. And that could make him even deadlier." He patted her thighs when the door to the bathroom opened and Aiden walked out. "Looks like your pool is ready."

She gasped when Aiden plucked her off Roman's lap and carried her back across the room. Since their tumble in the sheets, the boys had started acting like cavemen. Though she had to admit, there was something deliciously romantic about having them carry her. And she'd be lying if she said their possessive qualities didn't turn her the fuck on.

Aiden nodded as he placed her on her feet. "I know. You're quite capable of walking."

"I am. But being in your arms isn't completely bad."

"Glad there may be a glimmer of pleasure in there somewhere." He gave her ass a tap. "Get warm and don't come out until your skin is pink again."

She dropped the blanket then wiggled her ass at him. "Don't suppose you boys want to join me."

"Wench." He lunged forward, giving her a hard kiss before backing away. "We'll let you enjoy it for a while first. Water's too damn hot for us. I honestly don't know how your skin doesn't just burn off." He gave her body a long, slow sweep. "But once it's cooler..."

"I'll hold you to that."

He winked then headed out, leaving the door slightly ajar. She tested the water, moaning in pleasure as she stepped in and sank below the surface, leaving only her head resting above. She let the heat ease her aching muscles and purge the ugly images from her mind. Sometimes she really hated her job.

Minutes ticked by, the bath gradually cooling. She wondered when the damn water was going to be cold enough for them, when a muffled groan sounded through the sliver of space at the door, pulling her out of her thoughts. She glanced at the adjoining room, tensing when something fell to the floor in the next room, landing with a resounding thud.

Scarlet eased out of the tub, wrapping a towel around her as she tiptoed to the door. Damn, she hadn't even thought to bring her gun into the room with her, not with Roman and Aiden several feet away. But what if the killer had made the connection? Figured out she was a cop and had jumped the boys?

The inklings of fear cooled her skin as she took a deep breath, then shoved open the door. She stared straight ahead, her breath rushing from her chest. Aiden leaned against the wall, naked, muscles rippling, head pressed back as pleasure twisted his expression, his lips pursed together. His eyes were clenched shut. He'd tangled his fingers through Roman's hair as the man moved between his legs, bobbing up and down the man's length just as Scarlet had done on stage.

"Oh. My. God."

The words sprang from her lips and she hadn't realized she'd spoken until both sets of eyes turned in her direction. Roman pulled back, allowing Aiden's shaft to slip from his mouth, the heavy length held like a sword in his hand. His lips were wet and swollen, and just the sight of them caused liquid to pool between her thighs. A new bead of fluid eased from Aiden's slit. She motioned to Roman, moaning when he turned and licked Aiden's crown.

She drew a deep breath, trying to calm her frantic heart as she moved toward their outstretched hands, linking her fingers through theirs. Roman claimed her mouth first, a hint of Aiden's salty musk making her pussy clench in anticipation before he released her, turning her to face Aiden. He took her unspoken invitation, planting a hot, wet kiss on her lips before spinning her again and moving to her neck, nibbling at the sensitive spot behind her ear. She arched into him, meeting Roman's heated stare.

"I thought you two were going to join me once the water cooled?"

"Didn't realize we'd been that long. Sorry, darling. We'd be more than happy to join you now, unless we could interest you in another form of play? Though, I almost regret having to remove the towel. It suits you."

He snagged the edge of the terry, gently easing it free. It fell to the floor in a puddle of white, the tickling sensation of the cloth across her skin puckering her nipples into tight peaks.

Roman smiled, flicking his thumb over one hard bud. "God, I love how responsive you are. Looks like you're just in time to get dirty again."

She palmed his chest, preventing him from dipping his head and sucking at her nipple.

He raised an eyebrow, his dominant side bleeding through. "Scarlet?"

"Not so fast. When I came out here, you boys were already in the middle of something —"

"And now you'll be in the middle."

She thwarted his next attempt, this time dodging out from between them. "What if I don't want to be in the middle this go around?"

A hint of uncertainty flashed in Roman's eyes before he glanced at Aiden, who stepped forward, his naked body gleaming in the light. Slightly tanned skin over thick-banded muscles, just the sight of him made her stomach flutter with anticipation.

He stopped a foot away, brushing his fingers along her arm. "There something you need to tell us?"

"Just like a G-man to jump to the worst conclusion. It's nothing like that. I just have some questions."

He narrowed his eyes. "Such as?"

"Specifically? I've been wondering. Do you both..." She waved her hand at their erect shafts. "Give and receive?"

Aiden chuckled. "I didn't take you as the shy type, baby."

"I'm not shy, it's just... Fine. Do you both fuck each other's asses?"

"Roman prefers to be the one fucking, but yes, we both fuck each other." He raised an eyebrow. "How does that make you feel?"

"Other than the obvious aroused as hell?" She smiled. "I'd call it curious." She waved at the bed. "I don't suppose you two would be willing to show me?"

Roman moved in beside Aiden. "Pardon me?"

"You heard me, Roman. I want you to show me." She sauntered forward, trailing her fingers down his chest, scraping his skin until she circled his cock. "I'm still trying to wrap my head around how I fit into all this. I know you love each other and I believe you when you say you love me—"

"We *do* love you." Roman framed her face with his hands. "You're not just a toy to us—a convenient third, as you said the other day. You're our soul, Scarlet. What will keep bringing us home night after night. A fact these past weeks has made very apparent. We can't lose you."

"You're not going to lose me. All I'm asking is for you to let me share what you feel for each other. Witness the passion between you. You are going to continue to be lovers, aren't you?"

"Of course, and it's not like we're trying to hide it from you. We just wanted to wait until you were ready. We didn't want you to feel uncomfortable. We haven't really talked much about this aspect of our relationship."

"You know what they say—a picture's worth a thousand words."

Roman pursed his lips.

"I promise you. Watching you two boys pleasure each other isn't going to turn me off. Hell, I might come just thinking about it." She gave him her best smile. "Please? I *need* this."

The men exchanged a look, and she wasn't certain they'd conceded until Aiden tsked her, turning her around and urging her forward with a pat on her ass.

He allowed his hand to linger on the curve of her buttocks. "All right. But it'll cost you. We'll let you watch on one condition."

She gazed at him over her shoulder. "Name it."

"Next time, it'll be you between both of us."

She couldn't quite crush the soft rumble in her chest as she stopped at the bed, looking from Roman back to Aiden. "And will you be spanking me before or after you both fuck me?"

"Goddamn..." Aiden shook a finger at her. "You'd best get comfortable, baby."

Aiden sat first, flexing his abs as he leaned back, watching Roman retrieve the lubricant from their bag. She found the way Aiden's muscles rippled fascinating, showing off every inch of his firm body. He was slightly larger than Roman, with strong, bulging arms that held tight as he took what belonged to him. Desire had darkened his blue eyes, making them appear more like deep pools than the morning sky. He glanced over at her, giving her a wink as he lowered one hand, rhythmically stroking his cock.

The sight made her pussy clench and she wondered if refusing to be their third this time had been a bit premature. But the thought vanished as she watched Roman advance, his strong body a symbol of masculinity. He stopped in front of Aiden, batting the man's hand away as he slipped his fingers around Aiden's shaft, firmly pumping up and down the length.

"Don't you fucking tease me, Roman. It's been too long."

"Been right here the whole time, jackass."

Roman bent down, taking Aiden's mouth in a kiss so carnal, Scarlet's lips swelled in response. Damn, she'd never witnessed such an exchange of raw power before and the thought that they were hers…

She sucked in a ragged breath as Aiden fought back, battling for dominance, never truly submitting to the man. Roman growled when he pulled away, the gravely sound a clear warning.

Aiden raised an eyebrow, obviously not fazed by the outward show of dominance. "You're not the only one feeling aggressive." He swung his gaze to her then over to Roman again. "Watching all those men stare at Scarlet. Having that fucking photographer grope her while we stood there… I'm a bit edgy, too."

"Then roll over, and I'll fuck that tension right out of you, buddy."

Aiden sat still for a few moments, as if considering Roman's demand, before sighing and crawling into the middle of the bed. He acquiesced, but it wasn't a submission. The way he moved, the steely look in his eyes let Scarlet know he'd obeyed because he chose to. Because the act would bring him pleasure. Roman acknowledged the truce with a firm slap to Aiden's ass, making the muscles jump.

Aiden clenched his jaw but settled on his hands and knees, glancing at Roman over his shoulder when the bed dipped from the man's weight. His gaze found Scarlet again, the intensity in his eyes stealing her breath. God, did he stare at her like that when they were about to make love? Did his passion burn as hot?

He shook his head, glancing at Roman. "Our girl's doubting we want her as much as we want each other."

Scarlet inhaled roughly. "How the hell could you possibly know that?"

"It's written all over your face, baby. The way you scrunch your nose and worry that lip between your teeth. Then there's the slight frown." He gave her a stunning smile. "You can't keep secrets from us."

She huffed out a breath, toeing the floor. "I've just never seen you look at anyone the way you do Roman."

"That's because you've usually got your eyes squeezed shut. I promise you. What we feel for you makes everything else two-dimensional. And we'll prove that claim next time. But for now, stop worrying and enjoy the show."

Scarlet nodded, her throat too thick for her to get any words out. Roman kneeled behind Aiden, placing the lubricant on the mattress beside them. He unscrewed the cap, squeezing a small amount onto his fingers before tracing them down Aiden's cleft. A low moan feathered from Aiden's luscious lips when Roman circled his ass, penetrating him with a single finger.

Scarlet drew closer, watching Roman pump the digit back and forth, making Aiden's cock pulse. She'd never touched a man like that and wondered how it felt to be the one stroking their flesh. Roman turned toward her as she climbed on the bed, his lips finding hers. She ate at his mouth, her arousal so tight her clit pulsed. God, she'd never expected it to have this effect on her, but they were so beautiful—strong male bodies moving together in a primal act of desire—it made her feel dizzy.

She reached out, following the same path Roman had taken, smoothing her fingers across Aiden's skin. Aiden whipped his head around, his gaze meeting hers across his shoulder. She silently asked permission. A low rumble was her only reply as she smeared some of the lube on her finger and slipped it inside his tight channel.

"Oh God, Roman. Does it feel like this when Aiden touches you?"

Roman licked one distended nipple, making her hiss.

"Hot? Raw? Hungry?" He pinched one. "Oh, yeah. And soon, you'll feel it, too." He nodded toward his lover. "Add another finger, darling. I need him nice and stretched."

The moan that greeted her intrusion had her dripping juice, desperate to feel him come around her finger as she pumped it back and forth, reveling in the sporadic contractions that clamped around her penetration. She moved faster, loving how his ass clenched, daring her to withdraw, to deny him. A light sweat broke across his back as he arched under the attack, his thighs quivering from the apparent strain.

She glanced at his shaft, humming as it pulsed against his stomach, the head flaring in response to her touch. She moved faster, wanting to see that one moment when he gave himself over to her. Allowed himself to be completely vulnerable. But just when she thought he'd come, Roman stopped her with a firm hand across hers.

"You said you wanted to watch." He shook his head, smacking her ass. "So be a good girl and let me have a turn, or we'll stop and concentrate on that spanking we promised you."

Scarlet pouted but removed her hand, sighing at the sudden loss of heat. She thought about begging for one more turn, until Roman lifted the tube again, this time squeezing a long line of lubricant the length of his shaft. A dizzy feeling swam through her head as he swirled the slick fluid around then placed the head of his cock against Aiden's tight pucker.

"Oh. My. God."

The words emerged as nothing more than a raspy whisper, stalling completely when Roman inched his way inside, pausing crown-deep in Aiden's ass. Aiden groaned and levered back, sinking Roman deeper inside him.

"Ah shit, Aiden. Don't do that. You know I can't control myself when you fuck yourself on me."

"Then stop babying me and fuck me hard!"

Roman bowed his head, a hint of defeat in the hunch of his shoulders before he reared back, pulling all but the bulbous head free before pistoning forward, claiming the man's ass in one forceful stroke.

Aiden tilted his head, the cords in his next straining. "Fuck. Yes."

Roman dragged his cock out again, slapping Aiden's muscles with enough force the man shuffled across the bed as Roman drove in again, locking his balls against the man's hard flesh.

The act had Roman clenching his jaw, the vein in his temple twitching. "Damn, you're so fucking tight." He repeated the punishing stroke. "So hot and tight, I feel like my head's going to explode."

Aiden huffed out his breath and reached for the headboard, using it as an anchor against each forceful stroke. "Damn it, Roman. I said to stop babying me. Go. *Harder*."

Another slap landed on Aiden's ass. "Looks like Scarlet isn't the only one due for a spanking." He bent over Aiden's back, scraping his teeth along the taut muscle threading into the man's shoulder. "Maybe she'd like…"

Roman's voice keened into a strangled wail as Scarlet pressed against him, slipping one lube-coated finger down his buttocks, rimming his anus. Though she'd tried to remain passive, seeing the men move was too tempting and too fucking hot just to watch. Roman snapped his head around, releasing one hand from Aiden's hips to drag her closer, twisting her lips open as he thrust his tongue inside her mouth, mimicking the motion of his cock. She submitted, surrendering her body as she fingered his ass, reveling in his muted curse.

"Fuck, Scarlet." He squeezed his eyes shut, slamming his hips against Aiden's flesh. "So fucking good."

She moaned against his mouth as he kissed her again, forging her finger back and forth as she reached for Aiden. Her name bounced off the walls when she wrapped her hand around his cock, pumping it hard, using the slippery fluid leaking from the tip to ease her way.

His body tensed beneath them, every muscle flexing in turn as Aiden's head bowed toward his chest, his breath a raspy growl. "Fuck. Now. Finish me now, damn it."

Roman pounded into him, his motion blurring beside her as Aiden's cock stiffened in her hand. His shaft flared, contracting against her fist as he creamed her hand, his harsh shout rising above the creaking of the mattress.

Scarlet's heart thundered, her muscles tensing to the point of pain as she watched Aiden climax, his eyes rolling back in his head as his orgasm pulled him completely under. She fought for breath, turning to witness Roman's surrender when the man reached a hand between her thighs and pinched her clit.

"Yes." Her release caught her by surprise, the kaleidoscope of color flickering across her vision making her scream.

Roman echoed her cry, punching his hips forward as he locked himself deep inside Aiden, jerking his hips against the man's flesh. The heady scent of sex wafted around them, the familiar aroma easing something deep inside her.

Scarlet gloried in their release as she eased back on her heels, watching Roman hunch over Aiden, resting some of his weight on Aiden's body. She had every intension of moving back—allowing them both to catch their breath—when Roman pulled her in for one more drugging kiss. She gave herself over to the rush of desire, resting her forehead against his when he finally released her.

He nuzzled her nose, giving her a chaste kiss. "So much for just watching, huh, darling?"

"Could you have just watched if Aiden had fucked me in the ass?"

"Touché. But you'll still get a spanking for not following instructions."

"Sounds like I get a spanking for simply breathing around you two."

"That might very well be the case."

She winked at them as she raised her hand, licking the remnants of Aiden's release from her fingers.

Aiden groaned then pulled her down, sliding her between them as Roman eased free, plopping onto the bed beside her.

Aiden linked his hand with Roman's then draped their clasped fingers across her hip. "Get some rest. 'Cause once we catch our breath, you're going to wish you had."

Chapter Nine

"I don't like this. We have rules. We should stick to them." Roman crossed his arms, glancing at the other models as they shuffled through the door then disappeared into the studio.

Glade wanted all of the models to do some collective shots—without their partners standing watch. Allow the photographer more creative latitude, the older man had said.

Roman called it fucking bullshit and just another opportunity for Nick to fondle their girl.

Scarlet smiled, moving into his embrace. She wrapped her arms around his neck, lightly scratching his nape. "It's a group session. All the models are in there, not just me. I'll be fine. There's no way this creep can take out all of us together—not in the way he has been. Besides, I'm better than that."

"I'm not doubting you." He clenched his jaw. "But if anything happened…"

She nodded, leaning her head against his chest, seemingly content just to stay in his arms. He tightened his hold, trying to breathe past the thick feeling constricting his heart. Fuck, he hated this. Putting her life at risk when they weren't any closer to identifying a suspect than when they'd arrived. They didn't know how to protect her properly when they couldn't pinpoint any kind of concrete lead.

Aiden walked up behind him, raising an eyebrow in question. Roman simply closed his eyes. Since their encounters the last few nights, he hadn't been able to look at her without seeing his future — everything he could lose if he and Aiden didn't keep her safe. Didn't protect her from the unseen enemy lurking within the walls. And he could tell by the way Aiden had been shadowing her every move, the man felt the same.

Scarlet kissed Roman's chest, gently pushing back. "I appreciate that you boys want to keep me safe, but I'll raise suspicion if I don't go in there. *Alone*. Like everyone else." She brushed her thumb along his cheek. "I promise I'll be careful. I might not be the black belt Aiden is, but I can hold my own."

Aiden leaned in over her shoulder. "Which reminds me... When this is over, I'll be personally seeing to it your martial arts abilities improve."

She turned in Roman's arms, resting some of her weight against him. Fuck, he loved how she'd adjusted to having them both as her lovers so easily. How she allowed them to be strong for her without actually giving an inch. Though he suspected watching them fuck had helped ease any residual doubts she might have still been harboring.

She chuckled. "Sounds kinky, baby. Will we be alone when I pin you to the ground? Or does Roman get to help?"

Aiden moved, crushing her between them as he claimed her mouth. The kiss was savage, and Roman suspected Aiden was dealing with his own apprehensions regarding the current situation. Group or not, leaving her side felt wrong.

Aiden tapped his fingers against her arms when he pulled back, staying intimately close. "I know you can handle yourself, but shit...we promised not to leave your side."

Roman nuzzled her neck, needing to touch her skin, feel her breath. To her credit, she just went with it, wrapping one hand around his head as she draped the other over Aiden's shoulder, connecting them in a way only she could.

"Look at it this way. While I'm in there with five other women and the photographer, one of you can do a search of the dark room. See if the man has any damning evidence hidden away in there. And whoever doesn't go hunting can hang out in the lounge with the other guys." She looked at both of them. "We need this. It might give us a break. And I can talk to the other ladies without anyone else being around. Maybe they've seen someone watching them? It's been impossible to isolate them, what with all the parties going on. And with Glade's rule..."

Aiden sighed. "They're always with a partner."

"Which makes confiding difficult." She eased out of their embrace. "It's only an hour." She smiled sweetly at them. "You guys let this go and we can forgo the dinner Glade has planned immediately following and play."

"Tease." Roman huffed, reluctantly releasing her. "Fine. You're right. But watch your back. Just because you're not alone doesn't mean this creep won't try something. He's found a way to get to these women. Two together last time."

"Won't let my guard down for a second."

"Go. We'll be waiting."

She tiptoed up and gave them both a kiss then headed for the door, pausing at the threshold. Roman nodded as she gave them a smile, finally slipping inside. He ignored the voice in his head shouting at him to go after to her, shoving his hands in his pockets before he marched over to the door and beat the damn thing down.

Aiden shouldered up beside him, giving his arm a nudge. "She'll be okay."

"Damn straight, because you'll be sitting outside that door until she comes back out. And if you hear so much as a sniffle, you bust that fucking thing down."

Aiden glanced sideways at him. "Tell me...are you this possessive and protective about me?"

Roman chuckled in spite of himself. "You have three black belts and are a crack shot. Even I'm intimidated at times. And as much as I'd like to think I could kick your ass if needed, we both know you'd just be humoring me. But as far as possessive goes..." He turned and grabbed the man by the back of the neck before slapping a hard kiss on his lips. He thrust his tongue inside, tasting every inch of his mouth before easing back, releasing Aiden with a punch to the man's shoulder. "You're mine. Don't think otherwise."

"Good to know." Aiden cracked a smile. "And I might let you win, if the reward was worth it."

"Bastard."

"But I'm all yours. And Scarlet's." He scanned the area. "So I assume by your little speech that you want me to stay here while you go hunting?"

"If anything happens in there, you're the best at hand-to-hand fighting. I'm not too proud to admit that."

"And if you run into a problem..."

He smiled. "I've been sparring with you. I'm bound to have the advantage."

Aiden pursed his lips, his unrest palpable. "You're not the only one who feels possessive or protective. Watch your back. And remember to stay low if you are jumped — target your opponent's feet. Hard as hell to fight if you're on your ass."

"Yours is the only ass I want."

"Let's keep it that way." He rolled his shoulders as if attempting to release some tension. "Don't be long. No telling who might be roaming around. Just because this creep hasn't killed anyone other than the models doesn't mean he won't."

"I'll be vigilant. You just ensure our Christmas angel doesn't put that ass of hers at risk."

Aiden nodded, punching him in the shoulder this time before striking off to mingle with the other men gathered around the adjoining door. Roman made a mental picture of his lover, praying he wasn't leaving them both to face some kind of trap as he headed down the hallway. Glade had constructed a separate wing to house the studio, keeping it and the sessions isolated. Roman suspected the purpose was to further guard against industrial espionage, even if the items in question were proofs of naked women.

He cursed. That fucking photographer, Nick, had free rein over the shoot this time. And Roman knew Scarlet would do whatever was necessary to maintain her cover — even if it tore at her soul.

He fisted his hands, gathering back his composure. He wouldn't be much good to the team running around half-cocked about circumstances beyond his control. Scarlet was right. She'd been a cop for over a decade. She could handle herself and some slimy photographer if needed. Besides, Aiden was there.

He'd know if Scarlet felt threatened. Roman had no doubt that the man would feel it.

He tucked aside his emotions, picking his way down the corridor. The dark room was located at the other end of the wing and, with everyone else occupied, he should be able to access the place without worrying about others interrupting him. He paused at the next intersection, taking the hall off to his right. The left led to Nick's suite. He'd try there next if he had time.

The door loomed into view halfway down the hall, a telltale light hanging over the jam. Though digital photos seemed to be the norm now, some diehard professionals still clung to their film-based roots and he'd heard Nick Fitzpatrick was one of them. Roman checked each direction, removing the small set of tools he'd managed to smuggle inside. He jiggled the ends in the lock, moving them around until the bolt slid sideways, a soft click sounding in the hallway.

Roman darted inside, quietly locking the door behind him. He removed a pencil flashlight from his pocket, checking the walls to see if the place was alarmed, smiling at the blatant absence of security. Of course, the panel could be hidden.

He headed straight to the adjoining room, picking that lock before gaining access. He bounced the small beam around the space, settling on some proofs hanging over a counter. The images were flawless, the edges sharp. The guy obviously knew how to take a picture, though that didn't mean he didn't kill women as a sick hobby.

He studied the photographs suspended from clips, trying to place where each picture had been taken. He recognized a few from the studio, and some from the candid shots he'd seen the man taking in the parlor the previous night during Glade's little sex games. He growled when Scarlet's image appeared beneath the light, her silhouette impossible to miss. At least she'd had her back to the camera, nothing more risqué than her ass visible in the frame as she kneeled in front of Aiden. Though he had to admit, the girl was incredibly photogenic, her natural beauty more than showing through. Even with Aiden's fingers scrunching her hair, it looked sexy, the slightly messy locks just adding to the overall appeal of the picture.

He moved to the next, cursing under his breath. Another image of his girl, only the bastard had shifted to the side, catching a shot of her working Aiden's cock, her pretty lips stretched around his lover's girth. He had half a mind to take that one, but he continued down the row, silently vowing to burn the damn things once they'd solved the case. The rest were more glimpses of the various parties, none of which seemed out of place.

Roman searched the other counters then he headed to a desk off to one side. He opened a drawer, removing a collection of photos. He thumbed through the first few, stopping at a shot of one of the ladies standing with Glade, the entranceway in full view. He flipped through more, mentally cataloguing each couple. The man had definitely taken pictures of all of them arriving, though none was a match for the close-ups found at the crime scene.

He skimmed over another pile, drawing a harsh breath when he happened on a particularly graphic one. Seems one of the ladies was doing more than just posing in that room, and Roman wondered if her partner was aware of the affair. Not that sex was the driving force behind the murders. But it was a lead worth further investigation.

Roman placed the photos back in the drawer, scouring the rest of the room before leaning against the counter. Nothing. Not a damn thing to link the man to the murders other than the fact he had the means to take the photos and the ability to move freely within the manor without drawing attention. But so did every other staff member, not to mention Glade's security personnel.

He kicked at the floor, checking his watch. If he headed out now, he'd have enough time to do a quick search of the Nick's suite before the session ended. He started forward but caught his foot, tripping into a shelving unit.

"Fuck."

He flashed his light on the floor, shaking his head. A pair of purple lace panties. Most likely belonging to the lady noticeably missing them in the photos. He released a weary breath, taking a step before stopping short. A brown envelope peeked out from behind a couple of books, the edge just visible in the bright circle. He eased the folder out, opening the flap before shaking the contents into his hand. More pictures of the models glared back at him, only these were different. Something about the studio looked...out of place.

He shook his head, grabbing a few to study later. Hell, even if the creep realized some of his photos were missing, Roman doubted the man would make the knowledge public — or go to Glade. Not with some of the shit he'd get caught with. On a whim, Roman darted back over to the counter, exchanging the pictures of Aiden and Scarlet with others sitting on the surface. Then he rummaged through the desk again, taking some of the sexual ones as evidence. The angle of the pictures hid most of the woman's face, but maybe Scarlet would be able to deduce who the woman was. Either way, it was worth looking into, especially since they still had nothing concrete. He grabbed an envelope and tucked the photos in, slipping them inside his shirt before making his way to the door. He'd just opened the damn thing when the outer door rattled.

Roman retreated, locking the door before searching for a place to hide. He ducked into a narrow locker beside the shelves, holding the metal frame closed as he peered out through the slats. Male voices sounded in the other room, footsteps echoing through the walls. The lock clicked a moment before a large beam of light lit up the room. It bounced around the space, never staying on any one surface too long.

"There's nothing in here. That damn sensor must be acting up again."

The beam swung toward him, damn near blinding him as it centered on the locker. He closed his eyes against the glare, holding his breath as boots clicked closer.

The scuffing noise stopped outside the locker door. "I've told Glade to get the damn thing fixed, but he keeps insisting his tech guys know what the hell they're doing. Maybe there's a mouse or something?"

The other guy laughed. "Right. A mouse in this place. Whatever... Let's just lock up and check the other rooms in the wing, just to be sure."

Two shadows moved past the slats, then veered off toward the door. The light made another circle of the room, flashing off the locker again before the men left, their idle chatter gradually fading. Roman waited a few minutes then slipped out, opening the door and darting into the other room. He didn't waste any time, listening against the surface before cracking the slab open. More shadows lined the halls, but nothing sounded in the corridor.

He headed back the way he'd come, watching for the two security guards. He'd have to search the photographer's suite later, after the guards had found something else to amuse them. Besides, he'd been nearly forty minutes. Time to ensure Aiden and Scarlet were still where he'd left them.

His stomach clenched. Still no fucking leads. And other than a kinky souvenir of their time here, he didn't have much to show for his troubles. He only hoped Scarlet was having better luck with the ladies.

* * * *

Scarlet hissed out a breath, ignoring the way the Nick brushed his hands down her body as he repositioned her for the next shot. His fingers lingered too long against her flesh, and the way he grazed them across her nipples made her skin crawl.

She glanced at the other women, noting similar reactions from most of the ladies, as he moved down the line. Though a couple didn't seem to care that he got more than a bit personal. Either way, the guy was creepy, though that didn't necessarily make him a killer. But it certainly put his ass on the list.

"Okay, ladies, I want you all to smile."

He clicked off a few frames, dashing back over to adjust her hat. He gave her a leering smile, palming her breast as he backed up, supposedly judging his work. She fisted her hands at her sides, and she had to curb the urge to kick his balls back inside his body. Fucker deserved it.

He returned to his camera, calling out instructions, praising their every move. She followed along, biding her time, waiting to strike up more conversations. She'd already approached Ms. July, Amber Watts. The woman seemed friendly enough but hadn't shed any additional light on the murders. She seemed completely oblivious to the incidents, casually mentioning how unfortunate it was the other women had been busy.

Busy being dead.

Scarlet had kept that thought to herself, joining the others for more shots. Nick seemed to take an exorbitant amount of photos, the constant snap of the camera grating on her nerves. He'd already had two of the models remove their tops for some of the poses, and she knew the bastard would want them all topless, if not completely naked, by the end of the hour.

"Very nice." Nick straightened from behind the tripod. "I don't think I've ever seen such a sexy group of centerfolds before. Lord knows Glade can pick out the best tits and ass in the business."

He flashed what Scarlet guessed was supposed to be a provocative smile their way, but it only made her skin crawl more.

He laughed, the sound more than forced. "Unfortunately, I got so caught up I've run out of film. I need to go grab some more. It's just in the other room. You ladies hang tight and I'll be right back."

He made for the door, his pace almost rushed. The hairs on the back of Scarlet's neck prickled as uncertainty settled hard in her gut. Something felt off.

"Wait, Nick."

She darted after him, but the bastard didn't even turn around when she called his name, closing the door firmly behind him. She reached it several steps after him, twisting the knob as she tried to yank it open.

"Shit!" She pulled against it, the inklings of fear clawing at her.

"Scarlet? Something wrong?"

Scarlet took a calming breath, turning to face the woman at her side. Sarah Tate was stunning, with copper-colored hair and big blue eyes. The girl put most of them to shame with her easy beauty and charming personality. And as Ms. October, she definitely made witches sexy.

Scarlet gave her a smile. "Everything's fine. It's just…the door locked behind him. And I'm not fond of being trapped in places."

Sarah frowned, trying the handle as if Scarlet might have been wrong. "That's odd. Though maybe it's all part of their security?"

"Then you'd think it'd prevent people from getting in, not out."

Sarah's frown deepened. "I didn't think about it like that. But it does just link to the other main section of the studio. Maybe this one locks from the outside automatically."

Scarlet nodded. "Maybe."

Sarah tilted her head, openly measuring Scarlet. "You know, you don't seem like a model."

"That so?"

"The way you carry yourself. The fact you rarely come to the sessions with any makeup on. And how you're always observing everything as if you'll need to remember it later." Sarah shrugged. "You're just not like the rest of us."

Fuck.

Guess she hadn't realized how ingrained her training was. She'd been professionally suspicious for so long, all those traits had become second nature. And she'd be damned if she'd turn any of them off. Her instincts kept her alive. And her suspicions prevented others from dying.

She gave Sarah what she hoped was a convincing smile as she worked up a story in her head. "I guess you could say I'm a bit more...on edge than you guys."

She could tell by the way Sarah simply stared at her, the one line statement wasn't going to sway the woman.

Scarlet leaned in closer. "Before Roman and I got involved, I was trapped in this abusive relationship. Guy was a fucking monster." She raked a shaky hand through her hair, hoping the action would add to the authenticity of her story. "Anyway, when I was finally able to get away, I promised myself I wouldn't knowingly become a victim again. Took some self-defense classes, learned how to gauge the risk of going into a room just by standing at the door. That sort of stuff. I suppose it shows more than I thought."

"Does Roman know about this?"

She chuckled. "Why do you think he's happy I welcomed Aiden into the picture? The man's a lethal weapon in his own right."

"He's pretty damn gorgeous, too."

"Isn't he, though? And he's sweet, if you can believe it." She turned and rattled the door again. "He'll also go ballistic if he discovers they locked us in here. Alone."

"But there's six of us. We're not alone."

Scarlet nodded, hoping her uncertainty didn't show as she followed Sarah over to the others, fighting the urge to go back to the door and scream for Aiden. Not that he'd hear her being another room away, but...

She took a soothing breath—most likely she was overreacting. Allowing her paranoia to get the better of her. Like Sarah said—they weren't alone. Not the way this creep liked his victims. And Scarlet would give the asshole the beating of a lifetime if he thought he could subdue six women on his own.

Amber gave Scarlet the once over when she stopped next to her. "So, you have two guys now. Can't say any of us saw that coming."

Scarlet frowned. She didn't like the accusing tone in Amber's voice. "It works for us." She turned then spun back. "And frankly, what the hell? You couldn't *see* me having more than one lover?"

"Not because you couldn't get a second one, or anything, but..." Amber shrugged. "You're...different."

"How?"

"You're cautious. Intense. And you and Roman never participated in any of the games before. Honestly, I had you pegged as the undercover cop they said had infiltrated the estate."

"Funny. I thought it was Ms. February." Scarlet kept her expression fixed. "And we participated just the other day."

"So you did. And can I just say your newbie...Aiden..." She fanned herself. "Guy is hot." She arched her brows. "So, do the men..."

"Play? Oh, yeah."

"Damn." Amber sighed. "So you're not the cop?"

Scarlet grinned. "Do you really think I'd tell you if I was?"

Amber laughed. "I suppose not."

"Look. If there is a cop undercover in here, I'm sure he's just trying to keep us safe. You know, so we're not exploited or anything. Attacked." She rubbed her hands along her arms. "I don't know about you guys, but sometimes I get the feeling I'm being watched."

"Maybe because we are. All the time."

"I don't mean the games. I mean, other times. Like there's someone hiding in the shadows."

Amber's bravado faltered. She glanced around the room as if checking to see who was listening before leaning in. "I get that, too. At least, I have for the past couple of days. But every time I turn around, there's no one there."

"Are you sure? You haven't noticed anyone near you when you get those feelings?"

"No one that shouldn't be there. I've seen some of the other models close by at times."

"Which ones?"

"I don't know…Mary, Ms. September, maybe. Ms. November a few times. But I never catch them staring at me."

Scarlet squeezed the woman's shoulder. "Just do me a favor and trust your instincts. They don't usually lie."

Amber frowned, giving her the once over again when Sarah stepped in.

She wrapped her arm around Scarlet. "Scarlet was in an abusive relationship before Roman. That's why she's so paranoid."

Scarlet grinned her thanks. "And that paranoia is the reason I'm still alive and with Roman and Aiden instead of that manipulative bastard." She nudged Amber. "If you feel like that again, make a mental note of what or who's around you and let me know. I can have Aiden chat with anyone who's worrying you. He's pretty intimidating when he wants to be. Might be able to scare some creepy gawker away for you."

"I'll keep that in mind." She took a few steps away, glancing back at Scarlet. "Are you sure you're not…"

The door opened again. Nick strode confidently back into the room, gazing at them as if expecting to see something out of the ordinary. He headed over to his tripod, busying himself with loading the camera.

Scarlet walked over to the man, motioning to the door. "Are you aware the damn door locks behind you?"

He looked up, those cold, gray eyes clearly assessing her. "Excuse me?"

"The door, Einstein. It locked behind you when we left."

"Really? That's odd." He walked over, shoving the slab open before giving her a confused raise of his eyebrows.

She crossed her arms on her chest. "It wouldn't open. I tried."

"Any particular reason you wanted to leave?"

"Ladies' room."

"Perhaps it just got stuck."

"Or maybe you locked it from the outside."

Something flashed in his eyes, but it was gone before she could read him. "I'm sure it was nothing more than a misunderstanding. Can we finish?"

"I'd still like to use the washroom."

He stepped in front of her when she reached for the door, blocking her way, his hand cinched around her wrist. "We're nearly finished. All I need is another ten minutes or so."

Her muscles twitched, flexing as she fought the instinct to lock his arm behind his back and crush his face into the wall.

He increased his grip, stepping into her personal space. "Just ten more minutes."

She firmed her stance. "Fine. But let go."

He smiled, all teeth and thin lips then motioned to the other women. "Shall we?"

She huffed as he released her wrist then walked back to the group. Her skin stung from where he'd gripped her, and she had a bad feeling it might bruise.

Fuck. Roman and Aiden would go apeshit if it did.

Sarah gave her a concerned furrow, but Scarlet merely smiled, patting the other woman on the arm as she took her place. Ms. November bumped into her, somehow managing to scratch the same sore flesh Nick had hurt before muttering a token apology.

Scarlet forced a smile, mentally punching the photographer in the face as he clicked off more frames, making weird hand signals at them to shuffle them around. Amber moved in front of her, her short blonde hair bobbing across her shoulders when the lights flickered then died, blanketing the room in darkness. A few of the ladies screamed before a dull emergency light came on, casting a muted glow across the room.

Nick appeared through the shadows, his hands raised. "Easy, ladies. It's probably just a small outage. With the sporadic storms we've been having, it's no surprise and most likely just a temporary problem. I'm sure the power will kick back on any minute. Just stay calm."

Scenarios ran through Scarlet's head, the least of which had anything to do with this being a power outage. She glanced toward the door, finally discerning the outline in the heavy darkness. The fact Aiden wasn't already pounding on the metal slab meant that only the power in the damn studio had been cut.

Instinct took over and she lunged forward just as the collection of light stands and other equipment exploded off to their right. Glass splintered across the room, the tinkling sound rising above the chain reaction of screams. Smoke billowed out from the broken equipment, quickly smothering the room. She stumbled to her knees when one of the models slammed into her from the side, making the room dip. She palmed the floor when something hit her head, launching her face-first into the floor. Another series of screams echoed around her, then nothing.

Chapter Ten

Aiden paced the length of the lounge, once again glancing at the door leading to the studio. He hadn't realized that the actual photo location was through yet another door, and just knowing he wasn't quite close enough to hear Scarlet if she screamed his name irked the hell out of him.

He fisted his hand, stilling the urge to slam it against the wall. Roman hadn't returned yet, either. Just another fact that ate at him. While he knew his lover could handle himself, he hated the uneasy feeling prickling his skin—the one that usually meant something was off. And he'd learned to trust his instincts.

A noise rose above the din of chatter around him, and he walked toward the doorway, listening to see if the anomaly would sound again. It'd been too fragmented to place—nothing more than a ghosted echo that taunted his sanity. He stopped next to the door, cocking his head to the side, but nothing rose above the pounding of his pulse in his head.

Aiden palmed the wall, resting his forehead against the hard surface. He'd never been this protective before. Never felt as if his skin was being stretched too tight at just the thought of losing her. That he'd just sat there, waiting when she'd needed him. That he'd spend the rest of his life knowing he'd let her down.

"You okay?" Roman stepped up behind him, slapping him on the shoulder.

Aiden spun, pressing his back into the wall as he stared into his lover's eyes. Roman had a way of grounding him. Of making him see the bigger picture instead of getting tunneled down a single path — one that usually drove him crazy.

He motioned to the door. "I thought I heard something, but no one else seems concerned and it hasn't sounded again, so..." He shrugged.

Roman glanced to Aiden's left. "What does your gut tell you?"

"I never knew how much I needed her until she stepped into that damn studio alone?"

Roman sighed. "Besides that."

"That something feels off. But I can't justify it. Everything seems fine. And she was right. She's not in there alone. Guy would have to be pretty damn skilled to get six women at a time, especially when one of them is a wildcat."

"But your spider sense is tingling."

"Can't fucking relax. And I'd like to think it's from more than just the obvious. That I'm in love with you both and can't fucking breathe past the thought of losing either of you."

"You're not going to lose us. We'll catch this guy, and we'll leave here — *together*, as a family unit. Only way it can happen." He thrummed his fingers on his chin. "But I trust your gut. If it's telling you something's wrong..." He stepped back. "I say it's time for to check up on our girl. We can make up some bullshit story about her needing some medication or something if camera boy in there gets suspicious."

"Fucking A."

Aiden pushed off the wall, palming the door when the entire room shook as an explosion sounded in an adjoining room. The lights flickered then winked out, leaving nothing but a single sputtering emergency bulb blinking in the smoky shadows. The force knocked Aiden on his ass, bits of dust and paint clouding around him. He coughed, waving his hand to clear the air when Roman grabbed his wrist and yanked him to his feet. Shouts sounded around them, followed by the whine of a fire alarm.

"Shit! You okay?" Roman traveled the length of Aiden's torso with his hands, obviously searching for any injuries.

"Fine." He gave his head a shake to clear the ringing in his ears. "Stop worrying about me and get Scarlet."

Roman gave him one last quick glance then grabbed the handle, darting into the other room. Aiden followed suit, choking at the swirl of smoke. Shit, if it was this thick out here already, the studio had to be filled. Roman stopped at the next door, testing the surface before twisting the handle.

Screams rent the air as he wrenched open the metal slab, coughing at the thick cloud of smoke that rolled out of the room, crawling along the ceiling as it quickly expanded outwards. The man cleared the air in front of his face then clicked on a small flashlight before disappearing inside.

Aiden shadowed Roman's six, squinting through the blinding darkness in the hopes of seeing anything other than gray mounds. A hand grabbed his, nails biting into his skin. He caught the woman as stumbled into his arms, blonde hair hiding her face. He eased her upright, maintaining his hold as he brushed the strands from her face, Roman at his side.

"Ms. July?"

"Amber." She coughed, wiping the back of her hand across her eyes. "You're Scarlet's partner. Aiden, right?"

"That's right. Are you okay? What happened? Where's Scarlet?"

She choked back a sob. "The lights went out then there was this thundering explosion. I think the lighting stands blew. I don't know."

"Shh, it's going to be okay. Are you hurt?"

"I..." She sniffed, glancing around. "I don't think so. I..."

Roman joined them, bending closer to her. "Where's Scarlet?"

She shook her head, golden hair bouncing everywhere. "I don't know. She was behind me when everything went crazy."

"It's okay. We'll get you out of here."

She nodded, fear making her eyes look like giant white rings amidst the black. Aiden held her hand in his, when another woman emerged through the smoke, grabbing Amber's wrist. She tugged against Aiden's hold, nearly sending Amber to her knees.

Roman cupped the other woman's shoulders holding her steady as Amber regained her balance. "Aren't you Candi? Ms. November?"

"I've got her. You two go find your partner." The woman's voice sounded cold, distant.

Roman gave Aiden a quizzical look. "Thanks, but it's easy to get disoriented in here. We'll ensure you ladies make it out."

She sneered, tightening her grip on Amber's arm to the point the woman winced. "I said I've got her. There are other women in need of help. I can get us out. I know the way."

"Then you can lead, but one of us is accompanying you."

"You don't understand. I need her."

Aiden moved forward, an odd smell tickling his senses. It was sweet, but distinctly chemical. He inhaled again, but it'd faded into nothing more than smoke. "Are you okay? Did you hit your head maybe?"

Candi pursed her lips, backing down slightly. "I'd just hate to see anyone else get hurt. I can take Amber out and you two can search for others who may be injured. Like Scarlet. I saw her fall before I lost sight of her."

Aiden shouldered closer. "Where? Which direction?"

"It's hard to tell with all the smoke in here now. I think over there." She pointed in the direction they'd been heading.

Aiden glanced at Roman, recognizing the man's frustrated expression. One of them had to see the other ladies out. He gave Roman's arm a squeeze. "You go. I'll grab Scarlet and be out right behind you."

"Aiden..."

"One of us has to. I promise you. I've got this."

Candi shuffled her feet, looking as if she couldn't stand still. "I don't need—"

"You're not leaving here alone. Period." Roman nodded at him, taking both women by the hand then disappearing back toward the exit.

Candi resisted, her protests gradually fading as Aiden groped along, feeling his way in the darkness until his fingers brushed across the heel of a boot. "Scarlet!"

He shuffled over, tracing her outline along the floor until he could brush her hair back from her face, cursing at the bloody line across her temple. He placed his fingers on her neck, sighing at the steady throb beneath his touch. She was alive. Everything else could be fixed.

She groaned, rolling her head in his grasp as her eyelids fluttered open. She blinked a few times before she started coughing as she drew a deep breath.

"Easy, baby. I've got you."

She squinted at him, groaning again when she tried to move.

"Don't." He skimmed his fingers over the gash on her head. "Are you hurt anywhere other than your forehead?"

She frowned, dabbing her fingers along the cut, wincing as she drew it back and stared at the blood. "Yeah. My pride."

"That we can fix."

She hissed out a breath, palming her head as she coughed again. "We should get out of here. Are all the other women safe?"

Aiden sighed. "No way to know for sure. Roman just took Amber and Candi out. I haven't come across anyone else yet."

She nodded, groaning again. "We should look—"

"I'm getting you out of here. If anyone's missing, I'll come back in."

"I'm fine. Just a bit dizzy. I can make my way out."

"Fuck that. You obviously have a concussion. I'm taking you out. End of story."

She huffed but didn't resist when he scooped her off the floor, holding her tight to his chest as he picked his way back through the smoke, finally getting close enough to the exit to see the dim light from the room beyond the door. At least the emergency lighting was working in the rest of the wing.

"Aiden!"

Roman dashed over to him, grabbing Aiden's arm before leading him from the room. Smoke curled out of the studio, obscuring the upper half of the adjoining area as Aiden made his way into the lounge, coughing against the burning sensation in his lungs.

"Thank Christ." Roman angled Aiden against a wall, helping him brace some of his weight, before flipping Scarlet's hair back from her forehead. "Fuck, Scarlet, you look like hell."

"I'm fine." Scarlet shoved at Aiden's chest. "You can put me down now. Did everyone get out?"

"You're not okay. You were knocked unconscious, you have a gash across your head and I saw how unsteady you were when I helped you sit up in there. Bet my ass you'll fall on yours if I put you down."

"Smartass." She looked at Roman. "The other girls?"

"You were the last one. Nick brought out a couple. I got Amber and Candi, and Sarah managed to find her own way out. Everyone's safe."

"That's good…" She trailed off, staring up at him. "Nick? The bastard helped those women?"

"He was already standing here with them when I came out." He pressed a finger to her lips. "Can you just stop worrying about everyone else for a second? Shit, darling, we thought we'd lost you. I…"

He cursed, bending in to take her lips in his, the dominant possession of his mouth surprisingly gentle. Scarlet allowed him control, her body relaxing in Aiden's arms. Despite her fiery nature, she seemed to sense when they needed to be in charge. That by surrendering to their will, she wasn't giving up any of hers.

Roman pulled back, swinging his gaze to Aiden. Aiden hummed as Roman took his mouth, thrusting his tongue inside as if he had nothing to gain and everything to lose. Aiden fought back just enough to show the man he was equally invested — dedicated.

Aiden sighed when they parted, some of the tension expended in the kiss. He glanced around, noting more than a few gazes turned their way.

Roman stayed close with Scarlet snugged between them. He palmed the wall beside Aiden's head with one hand, the other resting on Scarlet's hip. He shifted his eyes slightly, not bothering to turn his head. "Don't care who's watching. You two belong to me." He looked down at Scarlet. "We need to get your head checked."

She gave him a sweet smile. "Yeah. For being with you two Neanderthals."

Roman tsked. "Talk like that is only going to get you an extra six whacks on that pretty ass of yours."

"Maybe your ass is the one that'll get spanked."

"Oh, darling, I'd love to see you try."

"I'm sure with the right motivation, Aiden would help me."

Aiden laughed, shuffling her into Roman's arms. "Baby, I have no doubt you could talk me into just about anything." He dropped a kiss on her cheek. "Go with Roman. He needs to assure himself you're okay. The firemen and paramedics just arrived. I'll wander around, see if I can pick up on anything." He pushed his hands through his hair. "I was kind of hoping Nick was good for this."

"But why would he help those women out?"

"I don't know. But if he isn't our guy, we're back to playing catch up. And based on this latest incident, we're way behind."

Roman headed for the far side of the room, placing Scarlet on a chair as he signaled to one of the paramedics. Aiden watched long enough to ensure she was being treated before walking around the gathering of people, asking as many questions as he could without completely blowing his cover. Though from some of looks he got, he swore he had the words 'federal agent' tattooed across his forehead.

Based on the accounts, no one had noticed anything out of the ordinary before the lights had gone out, though that in itself seemed odd. The power hadn't failed in the rest of the wing prior to the explosion, so the explanation that it'd been an unexpected surge didn't sit well with him.

Aiden waited until the area cleared before sneaking back inside the studio. Makeshift lighting gave the room an eerie glow, pockets of shadows stretched across the floor. He picked his way through the debris to where the light stands had exploded, squatting to get a better look at the remains. Broken glass and frayed cords littered the floor, bits of metal interspersed with the rubble.

"Not exactly how I envisioned this retreat playing out."

Aiden snapped his head around, cursing under his breath as Thomas Glade stopped several feet away, his gaze fixed on Aiden before seemingly scanning the room.

The older man gestured to him. "How's our Christmas angel?"

"She's with Roman. She has a concussion and a rather nasty laceration, but she'll be fine." Aiden pushed to his feet. "She was lucky. They all were."

Glade nodded, though he seemed distracted. "Yes. There seems to be a rash of unfortunate events occurring today. Just before the blast, some alarms were tripped in the dark room." He shrugged. "Security didn't find anything, of course, but... Perhaps the electrical system needs upgrading."

Aiden kept his expression neutral. "Maybe."

Glade smiled. "Either way, I'm grateful no one was seriously hurt. The last few ladies are with the paramedics now. Doesn't appear anyone requires a trip to the hospital. I'd hate for people to have to leave when things were just getting interesting." He headed for the door. "Wish Scarlet well for me."

"I will..."

He let his voice trail off as the man disappeared out of the doorway, not quite sure what to make of the conversation. He'd never considered Glade might be behind the killings, but now...

He reran possible scenarios in his head, heading out of the room. If he caught up with Glade, he could ask the man some questions—maybe catch him in a lie. Aiden stopped just inside the lounge, scanning the area. Other than two models sitting with the paramedics, the room was empty.

He made for the hallway joining the rest of the wing, hoping to catch Glade before he'd cleared the corridors, only to curse when the hall appeared empty. Either the man had ventured outside instead, or he was faster than Aiden had given him credit.

Aiden darted down the passageway, listening for footsteps ahead of him, when distant voices sounded around the next bend. He slowed, making his way to the corner as he strained to hear the exchange of words.

"Don't get mad at me…"

"Then make it up to me…"

"How…"

"You know how…"

The voices faded amidst hollow footsteps. Aiden peeked around the corner, nothing but shadows disappearing down another hallway. He raced after them, but the corridors were empty when he reached the next junction.

"Damn it."

He played over the fragmented exchange in his head. A man and woman, but the sounds had been too muffled to identify either one. And it wasn't as if anything they'd said had been damning. Probably just his nerves on edge after all that had happened. Worry over Scarlet and knowing the killer wouldn't wait much longer to strike again. And with Glade's security measures seemingly making a blitz attack difficult, the next kill could be even more violent. And might force the guy to deviate from his routine. Something psychopaths had a hard time copying with. Which in turn made the killer extremely unpredictable.

Aiden switched directions, navigating his way back to his room through the expansive house. Though he knew Scarlet was fine, his heart pleaded with him to hold her. Feel her skin warm against his, hear her heartbeat echo in his head. He'd meant what he'd said earlier. He hadn't truly understood how much he had to lose until she'd ventured off on her own, and he'd

gotten a shocking image of his life without her in it. Without Roman.

Over my dead body.

He chuckled at the thought. *Shit.* He needed to dial back the possessiveness just a bit or Scarlet would try to kick his ass. And with the way he felt about her, he'd let her. The key seemed heavy as he twisted it in the lock then swung open the door. Roman turned to look at him as Aiden walked inside, closing the rest of the world out as he shut the door. The man had their girl positioned on the bed, an ice pack covering the right side of her head. She leaned into him when he sat beside her on the bed, her gentle weight soothing something raw and primal inside him.

He dropped a kiss on her hair, giving her a slight squeeze. "How's the head?"

She tilted up to glance at him, wincing from the simple movement. "Sore." She huffed, twisting to point at Roman and nearly tipping forward in the process. "But I'm fine."

Roman crossed his arms. "Of course you are. The fact you damn near tumbled off the bed just trying to look at me backs up that claim."

"Bastard."

"But I'm yours, darling. Yours and Aiden's, and you're ours." He lifted his gaze to Aiden. "Paramedics taped the laceration closed and said she has a fairly substantial concussion. She should rest for the next few days and not be allowed to sleep for more than a couple of hours at a time tonight. He also told her to avoid contact sports for the next couple of weeks."

"Then it's a good thing I'm not a professional athlete. I'm fine, Roman. You act as if I've never been hurt before. Compared to getting shot, this is nothing."

A deep rumble sounded from Roman's chest before he bracketed her in his arms, holding her firm against Aiden. "Now isn't the best time to remind me of that. Not when I'm feeling this edgy."

Scarlet leaned fully into Aiden's chest, her head notched in the crook of his shoulder. She didn't seem at all fazed by Roman's mood. "That wasn't your fault any more than this was. Either of you. I'm just pointing out that I'm not fragile." She placed one hand on Roman's chest, gently scratching at his shirt. "And we both know you'd never touch me in a way that brought me anything other than pleasure. So you can ease up on the alpha male attitude."

"We should have been there. Gotten you clear."

"Are you referring to the explosion or the shooting?" She reached for his chin when he turned away. "Roman. Baby. I heard Aiden talking to you that first day in the bathroom, and he was right. The alternative would have been to let Everett kill you. That wasn't an option. Being in love means you have the right to make sacrifices. And I've loved you for a long time. Aiden, too. I just didn't want to examine that too closely." She drew him in for a gentle kiss. "I survived. Nothing more than a scar or two—"

"And half a dozen screws in a couple of plates."

"That's nothing compared to being able to share the rest of my life with you and Aiden. Right?"

The fight seemed to drain out of Roman as he glanced at Aiden, shaking his head before resting it on Aiden's shoulder next to Scarlet's. "How the hell are we supposed to win any argument when you don't play fair?"

"You're not." She groaned. "And I'm not too proud to say I'm tired and have one hell of a headache. Anyone up for a nap?"

Aiden kissed her cheek. "We'll both hold you. Glade's suspended the festivities for tonight, and all the ladies made it out of that studio in one piece. You can to tell us what happened after you rest for a few hours. Deal?"

"Deal."

Aiden helped her into the middle of the bed, easing back to stare down at her. "Damn, but you're beautiful."

She smiled and extended her hand, motioning them both to join her.

Aiden looked at Roman. "Which do you want, buddy? Breasts or ass?"

Roman laughed. "You know how much I love a nice ass, but I'll let you have the honors tonight." He smiled when Aiden's cock peaked against his pants. "Just don't get too used to it."

Aiden settled in behind her, one hand under her head the other looped over her and Roman. The man squeezed his fingers, the tension leaving his muscles. They'd allow themselves a couple of hours rest. Then they'd go over everything and find a way to stop this bastard from striking again.

Chapter Eleven

Scarlet sat on the edge of the bed, watching her men pace the length of the room. They'd only slept for a couple of hours, not willing to do more than take the edge off their fatigue before going through the evidence again. Though Scarlet could tell by the dark smudges beneath her lovers' eyes and the way each man kept scrubbing a hand down his face they were exhausted. And if they did figure this out, she knew they'd end up getting themselves killed if they didn't get some quality rest.

She placed her hands on the bed behind her, leaning back. "Boys. Look at yourselves. You can barely walk without bumping into things. I'm not the only one who needs more sleep."

Roman stopped moving to stare at her, one hand rubbing his temple. "We're fine."

"And that's why you keep massaging your forehead. You're both exhausted."

"You're the one who's been taking the big risks—"

"And you two have been with me every step of the way. Plus, I know one of you sneaks out of here every night searching for evidence. Or maybe you're just doing rounds to ensure everything and everyone's okay. Either way, you've spent even less time in this bed."

Roman dropped his gaze to her chest, lingering long enough to make her squeeze her thighs together to keep her clit from fluttering. "Maybe you're just too damn tempting."

She spread her arms wide. "Right here, baby."

He pupils dilated slightly, his eyes darkening as he took a step forward before apparently catching himself. "We need to go over everything again, first. There's got to be something we're overlooking—not piecing together." He glanced at Aiden then back to her. "Think you feel well enough to go through what happened?"

She scoffed at them. "I was well enough the moment you boys stopped carrying me everywhere."

"Right, and the fact you couldn't see straight and wanted to puke whenever you moved held testament to that." He sighed. "You are stubborn. But I feel a bit more comfortable with you working that brain of yours since it's been a couple of hours and you haven't lapsed into a coma on us."

He scraped a chair in front of her as Aiden claimed the spot beside her on the bed.

Roman rested his arms along the back of the chair as he straddled it. "Okay. Let's go through what happened. As much as you can remember."

She nodded, hoping the images had stopped shuffling inside her head. Truth be told, she had been pretty disoriented when she'd first gotten back to the room, and she knew the boys were right. She wouldn't have been able to give them many details, not with her head pounding and her ears ringing. But she'd be damned if she'd admit that to them.

She took a deep breath. "Everything started off fine with Nick doing his usual shoot. He fondled everyone's breasts while claiming to be repositioning them and took a stupidly large number of photos."

"Remind me to punch the asshole once we're done here." Roman straightened slightly. "So nothing unusual?"

She frowned, a nagging thought lingering just out of reach. "I don't... Shit! He left."

Aiden twisted toward her. "Say what?"

"Nick. He left." She licked her lips, rearranging the memories flickering through her mind. "He said he'd taken too many pictures...that he'd run out of film and needed to get more. So he left. But something felt off and I went after him, but the door wouldn't open."

Aiden gave Roman a concerned glance. "What do you mean it wouldn't open? Was it stuck?"

"No. It was locked. At least, that's what I believe. I tried the handle, but it wouldn't budge."

"Why didn't you yell for one of us?"

"Because I'm undercover! And if I'd started freaking out, the other models wouldn't have believed my explanation for being upset at the situation. As it is, half of them seem to think I'm the cop."

Roman pushed to his feet. "They know?"

She waved him back to his seat. "I think I convinced them otherwise — or at least that whoever the cop is, he isn't here to mess with them. But that's not the point. Nick left then came back about five minutes before the explosion."

"Did you confront him about the door?"

"Of course. But when he tried it, it opened. Which is why I think he locked the damn thing from the outside when he left."

Aiden frowned. "Why would the man do that?"

She shrugged. "I'm assuming he didn't want anyone to leave. He grabbed my wrist pretty damn hard when I tried to use a bathroom break as a means of talking to you."

Roman lowered his gaze to her arm, anger coloring his cheeks. "That's why you have a bruise? I thought you got it in the explosion? When you fell?"

"My wrist doesn't matter—"

"It sure as shit matters to us. What if he'd tried to hurt you?"

"Then I would have kicked his nasty ass. I only held back because I didn't want to blow my cover. And I doubt the other ladies would have bought me being a black belt like Aiden just a coincidence."

Roman huffed, carding his fingers through his hair. "Fine. We'll deal with the asshole later. What next?"

"The lights went out then the explosion occurred shortly after. And from what you said, Nick was the first one leading those ladies to safety."

Aiden held up his hand. "Can we back up just a bit? Where did Nick go?"

Scarlet divided her focus between them. "I assume he went to the dark room to get more film."

Aiden shook his head. "I was standing in that lounge the entire time. Man never left."

"And I went to his dark room." Roman grabbed a bunch of photos off the small table beside the bed. "Security paid me a visit while I hid in a locker, but Nick was never there."

"But why leave if he was just going to stand in that room between the film studio and the lounge? What purpose would that serve?"

"Maybe he wanted to set the charges? Get the women upset by being locked in a room."

"I was the only one remotely upset. And the explosions didn't come from the other room."

Aiden sighed. "Who knows? Maybe it's not even him. Just because he screams pervert, doesn't mean he's a killer. He could have ventured out to jerk off after touching you ladies."

Roman held up the photos. "Whatever the reason, he certainly had the opportunity to take the shots. There was lots of everyone arriving that first night, just none that was a match. I also found these."

Aiden shuffled over a bit as Roman placed them between Aiden and Scarlet.

She hissed at the image of her lips wrapped around Aiden's cock. "Bastard took photos of that?"

Roman grinned. "Aiden and I thought it'd look great framed on our bedside table."

She swatted at him, thumbing through the others. "Why didn't you show me these earlier?"

"Concussion."

She scowled. "You do realize that after this case is closed, I'll still be a homicide detective, right?"

"And we'll still be your lovers. Which means nothing is going to change. You'll be stubborn, and we'll be protective."

"You boys are impossible." She sighed. "So after everything, all we have are some sex pictures that don't appear to have been taken at any of the events, photos of me giving Aiden a blow job and these." She held them up. "This is the studio but something about it feels out of place. I just can't put my finger on it."

"I felt the same. But that's definitely Amber then Sarah in the next couple of shots. And they're wearing the same damn outfits they've been parading around in."

Aiden cleared his throat, looking oddly indecisive.

"Fuck. Aiden, buddy, I know that look." Roman nudged him. "Might as well just say what's on your mind."

Aiden exhaled a loud breath. "It's just... I know none of us want to consider one possibility that's been staring us in the face since this whole thing started, but..." He motioned to the pictures. "What if it's Glade?"

A cold shiver snaked down her spine. "Glade? But he's in his sixties."

"I realize that but hear me out. First, he has all their personal information. He could have easily gotten access to their schedules under the guise of arranging photo sessions for the magazine. He's the one that lost all that revenue from having the police confiscate those original photographs and he suspects one of his hand-picked models was a cop."

"So he kills all of them? For revenge?"

"Who knows? Maybe the guy is just sick. But people have done far more over money." Aiden shrugged. "He's the one person other than the photographer who wouldn't draw suspicion walking around here with a camera. And Nick wouldn't question it if Glade took some of his pictures. Might be why Roman didn't find any in the dark room. And Glade can go anywhere in the estate. Knock on anyone's door. Hell, if you really were a model, would you think twice about leaving the grounds with him under the guise of a professional lunch to discuss future modeling opportunities?"

"Oh, my God. And by coming to him for help, we ensured all the remaining models were assembled in one place. Virtually guaranteed him a chance to kill any or all of us without having to even hunt us down." She shook her head. "But, he's older. Those women were young. Healthy."

Roman grabbed her hand, lacing her fingers through his. "Very few women are like you. They don't know self-defense or carry Glocks. Sure, they could put up a struggle, but all the autopsies showed that they'd sustained some form of blunt trauma. I don't care how badass you are, a tire iron to the head is knocking you out."

Scarlet nodded, palming her head as pain flared through her skull. She just wasn't sure if it was the concussion or the case making it pound like a damn drum.

Aiden cupped her chin, gently twisting her to face him. "You should rest. Two weeks, remember?"

"Two weeks of not playing hockey or football."

A hint of a smile tugged at his mouth. "Scarlet…"

A loud knock drowned out the rest of Roman's words. He glanced at the door, nodding to Aiden before rising. He stuffed the pictures back into the envelope, tucking them inside his shirt then he snagged his gun out of the side table, holding it behind his back as he went to the door. He checked Aiden's position, smiling when the man moved in front of Scarlet before opening the door.

"Can I help you?"

A man with a thick neck and bulging biceps stepped into the room. "Mr. Glade wants to see you. All of you."

Aiden kept his weapon behind his back. "It's late and Scarlet's had quite the trauma—"

"Now." The man flashed them a forced smile. "Please."

"All right."

"I'll let him know you'll meet him in his office in fifteen minutes."

Roman closed the door behind the guy, turning to face them. "What the fuck? Since when does Thomas Glade have meetings with his guests...?" He glanced at his watch. "At ten o'clock at night?"

Aiden furrowed his brow. "Must be important."

"More likely it's a fucking setup." He nodded at her. "You said some of the girls pegged you as the undercover cop. Think they told Glade?"

Scarlet shrugged. "I don't know. I'd like to think we were all too busy to get chatty, but...it's possible."

"Fuck. I swear, if the man tries to kick us out, I'm dragging his ass to jail for obstruction of justice. Then I'll slap on a few indecent exposure charges and go from there."

Aiden walked over to Roman, palming his shoulders. "Easy, buddy. This could just be a casual checkup after everything that happened."

"Then why did he wait so damn late?"

"There were firemen, local police and paramedics swarming that wing. Sure, it was downplayed as an electrical malfunction, but that doesn't mean Glade hasn't spent the past few hours appeasing all the first responders. But just in case..." He glanced at her over his shoulder. "Did you bring any jeans and sweaters?"

"One pair. For the ride home. I was going to change in the damn truck the second we cleared the gates. Why?"

"Wear them. Make sure you're armed."

She gave him a curt nod, not liking where this was heading. Then she rummaged through her clothes, pulling out jeans and a form-fitting red sweater. The color didn't make her invisible, but then she hadn't planned to have to wear it during her stay.

Aiden's mouth kicked up when she emerged from the bathroom, hair tied back in a ponytail.

She looked around her then back at him. "What?"

He whistled. "Damn, baby, you look even hotter dressed. Those jeans...shit, they make your ass look fine."

"Talk about winning an argument... You boys can turn on the charm, too, when you want to." She removed her service weapon from where she'd hidden it amidst her clothes, tucking the gun down the back of her pants. "Ready?"

Roman sauntered over to her, skimming a finger along her jaw. "I don't know what's hotter. You in that red sweater or knowing you're armed."

"I love you, too. And I'll be careful."

"I know because you're not leaving our side. And if shit goes down, Aiden's taking you to the floor and facing your wrath later. If I wasn't worried about leaving you alone, I'd lock you in the damn room, but I'm sure Glade has a spare key."

"Again. I'm fine."

"Again. Stubborn. Stick close."

Roman led the way, noticeably keeping her between him and Aiden. The gesture warmed her heart, though it also made her want to toss them both on their asses. She'd managed as a cop for over ten years. She hadn't suddenly stopped being able to do her job just because they'd become lovers. As if on cue, nausea roiled through her stomach from the constant shifting of her vision, and each step made her head feel as if it was going to explode.

Aiden nudged her as they headed down the stairs. "You okay?"

Fuck, was she that easy to read? "Fine. You?"

"I'm not the one who looks like they're about to toss their cookies on the floor. Your skin is the color of the damn snow."

She exhaled, giving Roman a shove when he paused to glance at her. "I'll manage. But I won't lie. I'd be eternally grateful if there wasn't any running involved in my immediate future."

"Not if we have anything to say about it. Just don't do anything rash."

"When have I ever done anything rash?"

Aiden scoffed. "Every damn day, if Powell's reports are correct." He shushed her. "It's part of the reason we love you, but tonight just pretend you're not Superman, Wonder Woman or Thor."

"What I wouldn't give to have that man's hammer right about now."

"As long as you're talking about his actual hammer, we're fine."

She punched him in the shoulder, stopping behind Roman as they reached Glade's room. The door stood slightly ajar, the sight of the slivered opening sending a chill down her spine. Glade didn't seem like the kind of guy to lapse on security — especially after today's incident at the studio.

A hushed curse sounded between them as Roman drew his gun. He nodded at Aiden, motioning the man to the other side of the door. Aiden pressed his back against the wall, mouthing for her to stay behind them. She glared but nodded. They needed to work as a team, not have her worrying about whether her placement hurt their feelings.

Roman counted to three on one hand, shoving aside the door. Aiden barreled through, clearing the room with his gun as Roman flanked in behind him. She followed last, moving over to Aiden's right.

Glade leaned against a window on the far side of his office, tumbler in one hand, knowing grin curving his mouth. He raised an eyebrow at them, his smile widening when Roman holstered his gun, motioning Aiden and her to do the same.

Glade sipped at the brown liquid, swirling the rest around as he motioned to them. "Was it something I said?"

Roman took a few more steps toward the older man. "Your damn door was ajar. Who the hell leaves it like that?"

He merely shrugged. "A man expecting company."

"Someone set off an explosive device inside your estate. I'd have thought that would make you more cautious."

"As I'm sure you suspected, the detonation was mostly smoke. Nothing more than a few light stands and speakers ruined. Seems someone wanted a distraction." He motioned to the chairs in front of his oak desk. "Please. Have a seat."

Roman palmed Scarlet's back, placing her between them again as he slid onto the chair, watching the man on the other side.

Scarlet eased down beside him, hoping the constant pressure would stop the room from swaying. "How long have you known?"

"That you and Roman weren't what you seemed? Oh, my dear, I knew a day after the two of you arrived three months ago. While there was no doubt you were in love with each other, it was painfully obvious you'd never shared a bed, let alone any form of rambunctious sex. Though I can confidently say that's no longer the case — with either man."

Scarlet's stomach dropped into her boots, and she couldn't stop from gawking at the man, mouth gaped open, breath stalled in her chest. She heard Roman telling her to breathe, but all she could do was replay Glade's words over and over in her head.

She pushed to her feet, pressing her fists into his desk as she stared at him. "You knew? All this time you knew I was a cop yet you let me parade around in damn tit tassels and boy shorts! Jesus Christ, I got up on your damn stage and gave Aiden a blow job in front of thirty guests — and you knew? When the hell were you planning on letting us in on it? Why are we even here?"

Glade pinched his lips tight, glancing at the men before sighing and sinking into his chair. "Which question would you like me to answer first?"

"Don't patronize me. I want answers."

"If you'd just sit —"

"I'll sit once I'm convinced I don't have to punch that grin off your face."

Glade glanced at Roman.

Roman held up his hands. "Don't look at me. The girl has a temper. Always has. And I can't say that I blame her in this instance."

"Fine." Glade leaned forward, steepling his hands together as he rested his elbows on the solid wood surface. "As I told you when you arrived this time, I can tell impostors a mile away. And when I suspected you two weren't what you'd claimed during your last visit, I considered confronting you. Then I realized you weren't targeting me or my magazine, but rather the drugs I'd been trying to get rid of for some time. As such, I decided to see where you went with your investigation. I can honestly tell you, I never suspected Everett. Man had never missed a day of work." He snorted. "Of course, I realize now it was because he made more money getting my girls hooked on cocaine than through his photography. I guess I didn't screen my staff any better than my models. A drug dealer and a narcotics officer. But in the end, you did me a favor."

He sighed. "I'll admit. I fully expected to have federal agents on my yard by the next morning. When nothing every came of it, I suppose you could say I was grateful."

Roman edged forward in his seat. "If you knew we were undercover, why not just level with us and bring us in as staff?"

"Because no one else would have believed that. I don't hire men who look like you to wash cars or carry trays. Besides, you already had an in. And you needed to reincarnate Ms. December if the retreat was going to appear legitimate."

Scarlet paced across the room before turning and pointing a finger at him. "You still could have let us know—not pressured us to perform like your other guests."

"But that was exactly why I didn't. If you couldn't fool me into thinking you three were lovers, you never would have convinced anyone else. And I heard more than a few of the women talking. A couple had you pegged as a cop. I thought if you had to prove your cover to me..."

Roman crossed his arms. "So why now?"

"Because until a few hours ago, I sincerely believed this was all just for show. I never thought the killer would infiltrate my home, which is why I allowed you all to think your cover was intact. I figured you three would keep the women safe while your counterparts within the Bureau would hunt down this deranged creep outside of my walls. But after the explosion..." He shook his head. "Once I finished with the fire marshal, I had my security check up on the other ladies. It appears no one's seen Mary Clarke, aka Ms. September, or her partner since the explosion."

"What?" Roman pushed to his feet. "I personally talked to her—to every model. She got out."

"I saw her with the paramedics after I came out of the studio." Aiden pointed at Glade. "You were there."

"I haven't seen the young lady since. All I know is that she's not in her room and her vehicle is still in the garage."

Aiden shook his head. "This doesn't make any sense. She's not next in line and if we've learned anything about this bastard, it's that he's methodical and obsessive about every detail. Taking anyone other than Ms. July would only frustrate him. I don't even know if he'd be able to kill them out of order."

"Let's not find out if your theory's true." Roman pounded his fist on the table. "Damn, we still aren't any closer to having a concrete suspect. If Nick's the guy then why didn't he abduct Amber during the explosion? No one would have seen him with all that smoke."

"Maybe that was his plan, but it didn't work out. We showed up. Maybe he didn't think anyone would come inside?"

"No. He headed out with those women right away. He didn't even come back in."

"But if it's not him, then who? We've been watching every night. Security's high. No one's sneaking in and out of here without someone seeing him or her or setting off an alarm. Hell, I tripped one in the damn dark room, and I looked for it. It *has* to be someone already here. Someone connected to that first case."

Scarlet inhaled. "He doesn't screen his models."

Roman turned to her. "What did you say?"

"Not me. Glade." She faced the older man. "You said before that you didn't screen your staff any better than your models. That implies you don't screen the women. You choose them solely on whether they fit what you're looking for."

Glade nodded. "Basically. As shallow as it is, this industry is all about giving my readers the type of girl they're fantasizing about."

Roman grabbed her shoulder. "Are you suggesting the killer's one of the models?"

"Fuck!" Aiden slammed his hand down. "Ms. November."

Roman spun around. "What about her?"

"Remember in the studio, how she wanted to take Amber out? Kept trying to convince us to let them go out alone? Then during Scarlet's big show, she was scowling the entire time."

Roman nodded "Yeah. But neither of those facts proves she's the one."

"There's more. Before I returned to the room, I tried to follow Glade, but ran into a couple fighting in the hallway. I only heard a few words and I couldn't place who they were at the time, but it was Candi and Nick. She was upset and told him he needed to get her what she wanted."

"The pictures!" Scarlet yanked on Roman's arms. "Do you still have those pictures?"

"Inside my shirt. Why?"

"Lay them out on the desk."

Roman reached into his shirt and removed the envelope he'd stuffed there before they'd left. He shook the pictures out then spread them across the desk, turning to look at her. "What do you see we don't?"

"These." She picked up the ones of the couple having sex. "I knew I'd seen that tattoo before on the man's wrist. It's Everett. And I bet my ass the woman riding him is Candi. That looks like her necklace."

Roman held up the photo. "So Candi and Everett were lovers. Which means he probably had her strung out on more drugs than just the coke he was selling. So when he gets killed at the drop...and with another woman on his arm...Candi snaps. Blames the other women at the shoot for her loss."

"Or maybe she just blamed me — or should I say the undercover cop. But she didn't know which one of the girls was the plant. My name wasn't released."

"She doesn't know which girl betrayed her so she decides to kill all of you." Aiden shook his head. "Fuck! This is crazy. But it explains how she was able to lure the other women to her. She wouldn't have been a threat to them."

"But what about the sisters? No way Candi took them both out without a fight. Strong or not, she's not that good."

Aiden closed his eyes. "Nick's her partner. That might be why the victimization changed suddenly. He helped her kill the sisters and he was the one who violated them. That's why they were arguing. In the studio, I thought I smelled something for a moment. It was sickeningly sweet. I'm thinking it was chloroform. She was Nick's alibi. He helps the other women out, while she grabs Amber and no one suspects a thing."

Scarlet scrubbed her hand along her jaw. "But when you and Roman prevented that...he nabbed whoever was last to leave. Whoever had to wait to see the paramedics. By then, we'd all left thinking the threat was over."

Roman cursed under his breath. "This isn't good. People like Candi don't function like everyone else does. The rage she'll feel at having Nick bring her the wrong model? This could easily turn into a spree killing. She goes on a rampage with him and murders anyone who gets in her way." Roman pointed at Glade. "Get your security detail to round up the other ladies and get them out. Then quietly evacuate the estate. I'll call for backup—have a unit meet everyone outside."

Glade bowed his head. "I can't believe... I have cameras on all the exits. They have to be on the grounds somewhere or I'd have been notified that they'd left. And I doubt they climbed over an electrified fence."

"There has to be somewhere around here he could take her and be confident they'd have the privacy they'd need. After all, Nick thinks Candi will kill the girl. He might not realize how insane his partner is. So he's picked a spot where no one's going to hear their victim scream."

"The studio!" Aiden waved at them. "Think about it. Electricity's out. Alarms are down. And the only other person with a room in that wing is Nick. Maybe that's why he left. He was preparing a place to hide Amber in that adjoining room until everyone left and they could retrieve her. Then they could torture and kill her without being interrupted or tripping any alarms. No one's going back there tonight, not even security. No reason for them to. Everything's been destroyed that's worth taking."

Scarlet inhaled. "Those other pictures. That's why the studio looked wrong. It was from that first shoot with Everett. That's why Nick has them. He's going to recreate that shot, only to take pictures of them killing her."

Roman grunted. "So I'm going to go out on a limb here and say Nick is Candi's lover. That he's her submissive and does anything the woman tells him." He picked up a landline, motioning to Glade. "I'm calling it in. Go. Get your staff moving and get everyone out of here. I'll have agents meet you out front. Have a unit sent to the studio as backup."

Glade nodded, rushing out of the room.

Scarlet listened as Roman rattled off the situation, finally hanging the damn thing back on the cradle. "You know it might be too late if we wait."

"I know, it's just…" He pulled his lips tight. "Why don't you follow Glade? Ensure he gets everyone out. Aiden and I will go to the studio. You can send backup our way once it arrives."

"And leave you two to face this alone? No way." She held up her hand, cutting him off. "I'm scared of losing you guys, too. But there's a life at stake. And three is better than two, especially when we have no idea what to expect. Those crime scenes were incredibly violent. Who knows what she's capable of in that kind of state."

"All the more reason to keep you out of her sights. It's you she wants. And Candi might be fully aware you are the cop by now. Couple that with your head injury…"

"I'm not leaving you two and that's final. I can watch your backs if nothing else. But I'm going."

Roman huffed, nodding at Aiden as he headed for the door. Aiden waved her forward, sticking close as they ran toward the studio. Uncertainty prickled her skin. Damn, she hoped they were right, or they'd just given the killer the perfect escape and sentenced Mary to death.

Chapter Twelve

Roman hurried through the mansion, heading steadily toward the studio wing. Scarlet and Aiden shadowed his progress, their hushed footfalls in perfect sync with his. Shit, how had they missed seeing Candi's involvement? Though he realized serial killers were rarely women, it all made sense—in a weird kind of way. It also meant she was extremely volatile and unpredictable. While he knew that her delusional, obsessive behavior would compel her to continue killing in sequence, being confronted could change everything and unleash that anger on everyone in the room.

Memories of Scarlet lying on the warehouse floor, her blood bright against her shirt shuffled through his head—the remembered feel of her weak body in his arms, the pale tone of her skin as she'd bled out. He hated putting her at risk again, though he understood he couldn't prevent it. Couldn't ask her to stop doing what was clearly a defining part of who she was. But damn if he had to like it. And he sure as hell wasn't going to let her down again.

He slowed as he reached the hallway leading to the studio. The scent of smoke still hung in the air, tainting every breath as they stopped at the entrance to the lounge, taking stock of the layout.

Aiden shouldered up beside him. "Only other way in and out of that studio is an emergency exit door. But it only opens from the inside. Impossible for one of us to pry it open."

Roman glanced at Scarlet. "I'm hesitant to separate. Our best bet is probably to confront her. See is we can reason with her long enough to get a clear shot. I just don't see how we can sneak up on her or Nick, if he's in there with her."

Scarlet gave him a knowing look. "I should go in first. Talk to her while you boys come in behind. After all…it's me she wants. She might fixate on that long enough you can get into position."

"Scarlet…"

"You'll be right behind me."

"And if she has a gun?"

"She hasn't used one, yet. You need to stop thinking with your heart and do what you know is right."

"Never going to happen where you're concerned— or Aiden." Roman muttered a few words under his breath before huffing it out. "And for the record, I hate when you're right. Fine. We'll secure the area, and you can go in first. There's still no power, so all we've got is that damn emergency lighting and our flashlights."

"Understood."

A hint of fear churned his gut as he cracked open the door, clearing the next room as best he could visually before darting inside, gun leveled, flashlight scanning through the shadows. Noting appeared changed from when they'd last been there a few hours ago, the room still smudged with ashes from the explosion.

Aiden fanned out to one side as he took the other, allowing Scarlet to keep to the middle. They searched the area, ensuring they were alone before meeting by the door. Just one more small room between them and the studio. If they were right—and he prayed they were—Candi should have Amber inside, unless she'd already killed the woman and had headed out looking for another victim.

He motioned to his partners, slowly easing the door inward, wincing when it creaked. Shit. They didn't need to announce their presence. Surprise was their greatest weapon. Aiden darted through again, disappearing off to the left as Scarlet headed straight for the next door. Roman cleared the area to his right, staying slightly back as Scarlet crowded the doorway. A small triangle of gray light from the studio shone in the doorway, the slab obviously wedged open. Scarlet squeezed through as he and Aiden held steady at the door, a harsh voice breaking the silence.

"Ah, you're awake. For a moment, I thought you'd sleep through all the fun."

The woman's tone was bitter and low, a hysterical edge to it that made Roman's skin crawl. He peeked through the open doorway, but all he could see were shadows in the dull light. Scarlet waved him through, her silhouette just visible ahead of him. Aiden followed behind him as a muted groan sounded from the far corner.

"Don't move until I give you permission, slut." The woman laughed, the sound followed by a low thud and a whimper. "Whores like you belong on the floor."

Scarlet stopped, motioning him and Aiden to spread out. Roman moved off to the right, attention fixed on the woman squatting near a dark mound on the floor.

Her head was cocked to one side, a large blade in her hand. A camera sat on a tripod several feet away, another dark form posed behind it.

"Candi?" Scarlet's voice rang through the room.

The woman spun around, lunging for the floor, drawing the other body in front of her. Mary's wide eyes gleamed in the darkness, her head yanked off to one side as Candi held the knife to her throat.

"Easy, Candi, I'm just here to talk."

"You!" Candi practically spat the word out. "I knew it was you. All this time, I told myself you just didn't fit in. You were just too damn perfect!"

"Then if it's me you want, why not let Mary go? I'm here now. You can have Nick take my picture instead of hers. Wouldn't that make more sense?"

"No, no, no, it's all wrong. All wrong!" She rocked back and forth a bit, shaking her head. "I told him I couldn't do it like this. It has to be right!"

"I understand. You need to do things in order." Scarlet edged a bit closer. "I'm sure we can get Amber to come down here — let you take her picture first. Just let Mary go, and I can make this right."

"No!" The word reverberated off the walls. "You made it all wrong! You took him from me!"

"Everett?"

"He was mine and you took him from me!" She pointed to the camera. "Smile pretty," she mocked.

Scarlet tilted her head. "Nick? Why don't you come out here and help Candi make this right? You can take my picture if you want—"

Scarlet's voice cut off as the camera snapped a shot, the sudden glare of the flash obviously blinding her. Footsteps padded across the floor then Scarlet was down, the muffled sound of scuffling making Roman's flesh prickle. He darted ahead, but Aiden beat him to the couple. He pounced on Nick, yanking him off their girl before dragging him into the shadows.

Roman kept his gun aimed on Candi as she rose, Mary still snugged against her, shielding her. The knife sliced across the captive woman's skin, leaving a thin red line in its wake. Mary screamed, the noise muffled by duct tape across her mouth.

He matched Candi's movement, hoping to diffuse the situation long enough to get off a shot. "Easy, Candi, it's Roman. You remember me, don't you?"

"Stay back! I swear I'll kill her. Gut her like the pig she is, right in front of you."

"We both know you don't want to do that. She's not the right target, and killing her out of sequence will eat at you. You need Ms. July, don't you?"

Candi shook her head, the erratic motion clearly showing her growing unease. The woman was quickly devolving—overcoming her need to carry out her original plan—and if they didn't act now, she'd kill Mary before he could get a clear shot.

Candi waved the knife at him, scratching Mary's skin again. "I'll kill her. She ruined everything! Everett was mine! He was going to make me a star. But then she took him. Do you know what I had to do just to stay alive? What I let men do to me for money? No, she has to pay."

Roman cursed inwardly as her words sparked an idea. He shifted his gaze sideways. Aiden already had Nick face down and cuffed, Scarlet at his side, both their weapons leveled toward Candi. Scarlet glanced quickly at him, nodding toward the woman.

"But it wasn't Mary who ruined things, was it?" Roman eased ahead slightly. "It was Scarlet. She's the one who took Everett from you. Who made you do those things. Who took away your drugs. I can give her to you. She's the one you really want."

Candi's movements faltered before she shook her head again. "You wouldn't do that. She's yours."

"She betrayed me, too. She wanted to be with him. Let him touch her. Watch us. You're right. She should pay."

He twisted slightly, aiming his gun at the corner, not that it mattered. To Candi, it would appear to be in Scarlet's direction. "You heard her, Scarlet. You need to pay for what you did."

Scarlet shuffled over, holding up both hands as she slipped into his arms, mirroring the hold Candi had on Mary.

"See?" Roman edged closer. "I have who should pay. Killing Mary isn't going to bring you any peace. You need to end this. December's the last month. It makes sense to skip ahead to who's really responsible. The final month in the calendar."

The woman stared at them, alternating her gaze between the side of Mary's head and Scarlet. Roman could see Candi's indecision. The way her body seemed to twitch uncontrollably. Her brain was trying to compensate—somehow make the deal he'd offered her fit into her delusional plan.

She screamed, still shaking her head. "It's not right!"

"No. But it makes sense. Scarlet's the one you need. The one you should kill. You know you can't kill all of them. Not now. So who do you want to finish this with? Ms. September?" He scoffed. "She's nothing. Nobody. But Scarlet—she's Ms. December. The least you can do is finish off the year. She's right here."

Candi cocked her head. "You'll give her to me?"

"Of course. She betrayed both of us. All you have to do is shove Ms. September aside, and I'll give Scarlet to you. And I'll take the pictures."

She lowered her arm slightly, the knife pointing away when her eyes widened.

Roman reacted, releasing Scarlet as she dove at Candi, grabbing the woman's arm and reefing the knife away from Mary. He followed, shoving Mary aside then tackling the other woman to the ground. He grabbed her arm, knocking it against the floor until the knife clattered out of her hand.

Aiden appeared off to his right as he retrieved the knife, offering Roman a set of zip straps. Roman helped flip the screaming woman over, securing her hands behind her back.

"No. She's mine! I have to kill her. She's a whore. They're all whores!"

Her voice echoed through the space, the words becoming incoherent ranting. Aiden heaved her upright, spinning when beams of light filled the room. Roman glanced over his shoulder, smiling as additional agents filed into the room. They grabbed Nick off the floor where Aiden had left him then moved over to them, hauling Candi off, her voice still screaming out Scarlet's name. One of them wrapped Mary in a blanket, leading her away as more light filled the area.

Aiden kneeled beside them. "I'm afraid Mary's partner didn't fare as well. Nor Candi's. Looks like Nick might have killed both men solo this time. His body's over in the corner."

Scarlet sighed. "We were too late."

Roman cupped her chin, drawing her in for a quick kiss before shoving to his feet, taking her with him.

She moved willingly into his embrace, her heart beating with his, nestling her head against his chest.

He gave her a squeeze, resting his chin on top of her head. "We saved Mary. That's something. And the rest of the models." He tilted his head over to look at her. "I wasn't sure you were going to like my idea."

"You mean the one where you offered to hand me over to her?" She snorted. "I'm thankful you never actually pointed your gun at me. That would have been grounds for a thorough ass-kicking."

"You could sure as hell try, darling."

"I have Aiden on my side. I don't have to try."

Roman eased back. "He's my lover, too. What makes you think he'll side with you?"

"Because I'm way cuter than you. And he wants my ass."

"He's not the only one."

Roman looked up when one of the agents walked over, muttering about someone wanting to see them then waving at the doorway. He eased Scarlet away, taking her hand in his as he walked toward the entrance, Aiden behind him. They ducked under the yellow tape one of the other agents had strung then headed for the older man standing in the lounge.

Glade extended his hand. "Congratulations. I see you caught Ms. November and her accomplice. I suppose this means I can rest easy, knowing the remaining models are what they appear to be?"

"No promises there. Women are seldom that simplistic." Roman shook the man's hand. "Thanks for acting when you did, or this would have turned out as another bloody crime scene. Who knows if she would have even stuck around? We could have spent the next few months tracking her down, one dead body after another. And she would have kept killing. Of that, I have no doubts."

Scarlet punched him in the shoulder. "Don't be so nice. I'm still pissed he knew and never let on."

Glade smiled. "Something tells me that maybe what you're really upset about is that you've discovered you're quite an exhibitionist at heart."

She snorted. "Not exactly what's running through my head, but..."

"Well, if you ever change your mind, give me a call. I assume the Feds will abscond with this round of pictures, as well. But if you ever decide police work isn't for you..."

A brilliant smile lifted her mouth. "Are you offering me a job as a model?"

"I'd be a fool not to. And I stand by my original decision. You make a beautiful Christmas angel." He stepped back. "Feel free to stay as long as you'd like — minus the pressure to join in any of the 'reindeer games'. The room is yours."

Scarlet rolled her eyes as Glade headed toward Mary. "Can you believe that?"

Aiden shrugged. "You do make a sexy angel, baby."

"I meant the part where he thinks a bit of flattery is going to gain him forgiveness..."

Aiden wrapped his arm around her shoulders. "I think that man is smarter than we ever gave him credit." His expression sobered. "How's your head? Fuck, when Nick grabbed you..."

"That damn camera flash was like a flash bang going off. Couldn't see a damn thing. But you were on him."

"Not until he'd tackled you to the floor. And I'm betting he knocked your head again."

"I'm fine, Aiden. Let's just concentrate on being happy this case is over."

"I don't know, baby. I think Glade was on to something. I think you like being on center stage."

She whacked him in the chest. "In the center maybe. But not on stage." She tugged Aiden's hand. "Can we just go, now? I really would like to get some sleep."

"You want to stay here or head home?"

She glanced at Roman, indecision creasing her brow.

He stepped forward, taking her other hand. "Darling? Everything okay?"

"Fine. I was just thinking…"

"What?"

"That I like the sound of that. Home."

"Us, too. So which is it going to be?"

"If you two are up for the drive… Let's go home. I'd like to wake up with you two in our own bed."

"Deal. Just be forewarned. You'd best get some rest because Aiden and I have plans. We still haven't been together the way we've dreamed about, and as soon as we're sure you're not seeing double, you'll be feeling it."

Chapter Thirteen

Scarlet hummed, blinking her eyes open, squinting in an effort to bring the room into focus. Dull light streamed in from the window, the long shadows on the floor suggesting she'd slept late. All afternoon if her guess was right.

She sat up, palming her head as the bed seemed to flip-flop. She vaguely remembered Aiden carrying her in from the truck and being sandwiched between the two men all night. Roman had woken her more than a few times to ask a few questions, then kissed her asleep again. And she'd apparently slept the day away.

"I know that look, buddy. Our girl is plotting."

She shifted her gaze at the sound of Roman's voice, smiling at the two men standing in the doorway. Chests bare, jeans slung low, they could have been models from any men's magazine. And they were *hers*.

They sauntered over, each going to a different side of the bed. She watched them move, muscles contracting, flesh rippling. They were beyond handsome. But it was what hid beneath their skin that touched her heart the most. Their trust, their obvious pride.

Roman sat on the edge of the bed, dipping the mattress slightly. He traced his finger along her cheek, skimming it over the bandage on her forehead. "How do you feel?"

"I'm fi..." She sighed.

Roman had trusted her enough to use her as bait. He and Aiden deserved more than just token answers.

"My head hurts. The room still looks like a damn tilt-a-whirl."

Roman raised an eyebrow. "Honesty? How refreshing."

She swatted at his chest, resisting the moan that bubbled in hers as her hand connected with hard, warm flesh. "Bastard."

"So you keep saying." He snagged her fingers before she could pull them back, holding it against him. "I'm just surprised. I'd expected you to lie." He raised his other hand in apology. "Sorry...downplay."

"I just figured after your show of faith yesterday, you both deserved more."

He clenched his jaw. "If you're referring to being part of the ploy, I'm still not happy with my decision. Thankfully, it all worked out."

"I'm not fragile. Still a homicide detective. You boys are still G-men. We have to trust the others to make good choices out in the field. And whether you boys like it or not, you're not my keeper."

"Aiden's not the issue. You're the one who seems to think you're bulletproof, despite evidence to the contrary. And we *are* your keepers. We told you we love you. That grants us certain rights."

"Then it follows that I have the same rights."

He smiled in a way that make her want to fuck him and punch him at the same time. "Afraid it doesn't quite work that way, darling, but if you need to believe it does…"

"Sounds like I might need to give you an ass kicking, after all. To prove my place in the pack."

"Oh, we have plans for your ass, but it has nothing to do with kicking. As a matter of fact…" He nodded at Aiden, smiling when he slipped in behind her, dragging her against his chest. "If you feel up to it, I think it's time we showed you just how much we love you. What your life means to us."

"But…" Her gaze met Roman's.

Despite the playful bantering, he looked scared and, for the first time, she saw the case through their eyes. How she would have felt if someone had been stalking them instead of her. If their fate had become a carved up photo in a file on a desk. And just thinking about it made her stomach heave.

She surrendered, lifting her arms as Aiden reached for the hem of the shirt they'd tossed on her last night, tilting her head as he pulled it over and off her then throwing it aside. He rose from the bed, shucked his pants then reclaimed his place, tracing a path down her body, caressing each inch of skin. It was then she realized this wasn't just sex. It was a loving—a physical show of their commitment. She let her head fall back on his shoulder, savoring how he pulled her against him, rubbing his flesh across hers. He was always so warm and she loved how he touched her until their temperatures matched. Who was she kidding? She loved him—them. And she would until the day she died. They were more than partners. They completed her.

"You're so beautiful." Roman stood then slowly removed his pants before offering her his hand. "Everett was right. You're the perfect Christmas angel." He tugged her onto her knees before leaning forward and tasting her lips with a fleeting kiss. "We'll do this nice and slow. Just know this. Once we're finished, you won't want us to set you free."

"I already don't." She glanced over her shoulder at Aiden, noting how his eyes had narrowed and his lips had turned up at the edges. She looked at Roman. "And I don't need slow."

"And the fact you said the room's still spinning?"

"Won't matter when I close my eyes." She turned into Aiden as he pressed against her back and nipped at his lip, knowing he loved the touch of pain as much as she did. "I need more than just a gentle fuck. I need you both to love me like you'll never let me go."

The men exchanged a heated glance before Aiden tucked her against his chest and scooted over until he rested against the headboard, her body nestled between his legs. He looped his feet under her knees, splaying her thighs wide as Roman crawled onto the bed and settled between them.

He placed his hand on her mound, drawing a finger through her slit. "Fuck, darling. You're already wet."

"You mean still. I'm still wet from the last time you boys loved me." She smiled. "Thinking I'm going to end up ruining more than a few pairs of pants from wanting you both all the time."

"I'm certain we can come to an arrangement that will save your pants." He lowered onto his elbows, tucking his hands under her thighs and lifting her pussy toward his face. "No teasing this time. We need you too much."

"God, Roman."

Her breath hissed free as he buried his face in her crotch, licking and nipping at her sex. Aiden lowered one hand, spreading her wet folds apart, flicking his finger across her clit. Pleasure shot through her groin, coiling quickly in her belly as they launched her hard toward release. God, it'd only been a minute and she could feel her stomach fluttering, her skin warming as her orgasm swelled inside her. No slow ascent or subtle touches. This was no holds barred, zero to a hundred.

Aiden bit at her earlobe, moving his lips along her neck. "Shit, I can feel you starting to pulse already. Damn, I love we can drive you mad in seconds."

"Two against one... Oh, God." She sucked in a quick breath. "Not fair."

"Fair's for wussies." He licked her skin. "But mark my words. Next time, you're getting that spanking we've been promising you. And you'll come hard and fast with my fingers inside your ass as Roman peppers your skin with his hand."

"Fuck, Aiden."

She rocked her head against his chest, barely holding on as Roman sank two fingers inside her channel, thrusting them back and forth. Aiden growled against her neck, sliding his other hand under her hip, joining his finger with Roman's before moving to her ass. His firm penetration pushed her higher and she held her breath as she quivered on the edge—her muscles clenching in anticipation. The boys held her there, waiting, until Roman latched to her clit and sucked.

"Yes."

She hissed through her release, raising her hips to meet their penetration. The men kept moving, claiming her pussy and ass until she collapsed against Aiden—spent.

Roman eased up from between her thighs, his lips glistening with her climax. Aiden speared his hand through Roman's hair, dragged him to him then claimed the man's mouth in a brutal kiss.

"God, please tell me you boys are going to fuck again, because damn...just the thought is driving me crazy."

Roman pulled back. Knowing Aiden had licked the evidence of her release off Roman's mouth had Scarlet whimpering as her pussy clenched around the emptiness.

Roman leaned down, hovering his face next to hers, the scent of her orgasm surrounding her. "Naughty wench. This time's about you."

"You can claim my ass while Aiden takes yours."

He closed his eyes on a grunt, the vein at his temple pulsing. He took a ragged breath then reacted, helping Aiden spin her around, her hands and knees once again hitting the mattress. Aiden shuffled beneath her, straddling her legs around his thighs as his cock pulsed against her groin.

Roman crawled in behind her, jerking her head back with a sharp tug of her hair. "You told us you wanted us to love you like we would never let you go and we intend to do that—and more."

He nipped at her neck, slapping his hand across her ass. Damn, why did the pain feel so good?

Aiden cupped her waist, drawing small circles across her hips with his thumbs. "We were going to spend hours worshiping you. Licking your sweet pussy over and over, building you up slowly. But, damn, when you talk like that." He wrapped one hand around her back, pulling her forward. "Guess we'll do that next time. Now place those lovely breasts against my chest while Roman gets you ready."

Scarlet moved with him—certain his grip would've shifted her regardless—and laid her body on his, moaning out at the sensual way he drew patterns along her back. Aiden smiled against her hair, dropping a quick kiss on it.

"Do you know how hard it's been touching you without taking you like this?" His breath rustled her hair as he blew out in a long sigh. "Just watching Roman get the lube makes me want to thrust into you. Damn, I can't wait until it's my turn."

Scarlet tilted her chin, meeting his gaze. "Roman doesn't have to be first."

Aiden smiled and reached for her cheek, drawing his hand along the curve. "That's very sweet, baby. But I know how long Roman's been waiting to love you this way. And seeing as I love him, too… But I'll have you next. Make no mistake about that."

She smiled and caught his finger in her mouth as he traced her lips, sucking it inside with the same motion she'd used to drain him that first time. He groaned and punched his hips up, sliding his length through her slit, her moisture coating his skin. She matched his motion, brushing his cock against her clit, closing her eyes as her nub pulsed. She'd never responded so quickly before, going from hopeful to horny in a heartbeat, with coming full force after that. But just feeling Roman tracing the curve of her ass as she rode Aiden's cock had another release hinging on the edge, one touch away from exploding.

"You've got the most amazing ass." Roman massaged her skin, easing some of the nerves fluttering her stomach. "I've been dreaming about this since that first time on the bearskin rug, but there was something missing."

Aiden glided his hands with Roman's.

"It's not missing anymore." Roman leaned forward, licking her earlobe. "I'm going to enter you first. Let you get used to the sensation of having me inside you. Then Aiden will join us. You'll be full of us. So damn full you won't be able to tell which part of your body belongs to you, because it belongs to us. We told you... You're our soul and we'll prove it." He eased back, keeping one hand pressed between her shoulder blades. "Stay just like this, and trust me not to hurt you."

Scarlet shot him a quick glance over her shoulder, licking Aiden's nipple as she anchored her hands around the man's shoulder. The smile she flashed him ended with a resounding smack to her ass, making the juice flow from her slit. She squeezed her eyes shut.

"I suggest you rein in that saucy attitude, or I'll spank your ass red before I fuck it."

He landed another whack, slightly harder. She tried to find anger at his dominance, but her clenching pussy begged for more. Roman chuckled and smoothed his hand over her flesh.

"Never knew the pain could be so hot, did you?" He moaned, sinking two broad fingers inside her sex, building her need. "Just wait. This is going to be blow your mind."

"Oh, God!"

Her voice sounded husky and raw, as if it'd been dragged from deep within her, as Roman circled her anus, easing his slippery finger past her tight muscles and sinking it inside her. She tried not to hunger for the impalement but couldn't stop herself from thrusting back when he retreated. Roman grunted and plunged again.

"Damn. You're so fucking tight." He added a second finger, the slight burn of his penetration making her hiss. "Can you feel how badly your body wants me inside you? Every inch is clinging to my fingers, begging me to give you more." He removed his hand then smeared more lube against her pucker, spreading it around, coating her walls with the slick fluid. "Okay, darling, I can't wait any longer. Try to relax."

Scarlet wanted to loosen up, but the tight press of his cock against her tender hole had her tensing. Aiden shifted beneath her, pulling her closer, capturing her lips as he danced his fingers through her slit, swirling juice around her clit. She cried into his mouth, losing herself in his intimate caress as Roman tried again, pulling her cheeks apart, pressing his crown against her hole. There was a moment of intense pressure before his cock slipped inside. He stopped, the thick head lodged tight.

Her cry was dark, deep, keening into a hungry wail as he surged forward, burying himself to the hilt.

"Fuck, Aiden. Get you cock inside her before I cream her ass."

Aiden released her mouth, angling her hips slightly. She was full—so full of Roman she couldn't see how Aiden would fit. She stilled when he swirled his cock around her sex, coating it with her cream. She unclenched her eyes long enough to look at him, stunned by the love in his gaze as he lodged his cockhead at her entrance, pulling her onto him in one strong thrust.

She screamed. There was no other way to express the sheer pleasure and pain coursing through her. Aiden's hard entrance sent her pussy into a spasm. She rubbed her mound against him, the rough pass of his skin against her clit sending her into an orgasm. She reared up, arching around two sets of male hands, her body exploding into a thousand pinpoints of light.

She couldn't open her eyes, couldn't move as they started up a gentle rhythm, countering their thrusts, filling one channel then the next. Colors blurred across her vision, sounds she didn't recognize floating in her head as their bodies became one—a writhing mass of flesh and muscle.

Roman called out behind her, twisting her hair around his fingers, tugging on it as if it would save him from falling into the abyss. She locked her hands around Aiden's shoulders, knowing she was scratching his flesh but unable to stop. They were thrusting together now, claiming her body as one then leaving it empty, wanting. She tried to shout, to beg them not to leave, but she couldn't get her voice to do more than moan. Pleasure and pain became one, the sharp sting of Roman's cock up her ass shadowed by the sheer ecstasy of Aiden's shaft in her pussy. She arched farther, unable to control her release, but desperate for it to shatter her. They moved faster when her body trembled, tears washing down her cheeks.

A wail of sexual bliss was the only indication she'd climaxed. Their names swirled in her head, but she didn't have the strength to whisper them. Somewhere in the distance, her name joined theirs, their cocks thickening until she wondered how they kept moving. Then they were jerking into her, their combined releases hot against her sensitive flesh.

"Scarlet! Oh, God. So good...so fucking good, baby." Aiden pressed his hips against her thighs, keeping him lodged deep as he continued to empty himself inside her.

Aiden and Roman possessed her, their words lingering in the air. All she knew was the beat of their hearts echoing in her head, the realization that they'd made her feel complete when she hadn't even known she'd been empty.

Aiden ran a shaky hand down her back, drawing her close, whispering sweet words as Roman eased his weakening flesh from her body. She moaned at the loss of contact, humming softly when he collapsed beside her, rolling her onto her side, cradling her body between them.

"Scarlet? Baby, are you okay?"

Roman's voice, or was it Aiden's? It didn't matter. Her words were meant for both. "I love you."

"Ditto, darling. Just answer us one thing. Are you still thinking about kicking our asses?"

She laughed, somehow prying open her eyes. "Just let me catch my breath."

"Wench." Roman flopped onto his back, helping her lay across his arm as Aiden placed his hand over her hips. "So about the living arrangements..."

She sighed, burrowing her ass against Aiden's groin, grinning at his hushed curse as his cock jerked against her flesh. "Something wrong with this?"

"We just weren't sure if you'd want us to move in. We both have places, too, if you'd prefer."

She chuckled. "Is that your way of saying I can keep my house as an 'out', should I ever feel I need it?"

Aiden tapped her ass. "No. We're just trying not to push you too fast. Leave that decision up to you."

"Aiden. You boys both have one-room apartments. If we move into one of them, where will our kids sleep?"

Aiden pressed onto his elbow, his mouth hinged open as he stared down at her. "Our. Kids?"

"Not right away, but eventually." She glanced at Roman. "You both do want kids, don't you?"

"Hell, yeah, it's just…" He shrugged. "We weren't sure you'd want to take the time off. Being a cop—"

"Isn't nearly as important as being a family. And that's what we are—a family."

"Yes, ma'am."

"But I'm still a cop. Five kids aside, that's not going to change."

"Five?" Roman chuckled as he settled beside her again. "So the fact you're relaxed and happy… Would now be a good time to tell you you're this month's centerfold for Spyce Magazine?"

"What?" She bolted up, only to have Aiden pull her back down. "But I thought…"

"That original shoot, remember?" Roman patted her arm. "Don't worry. We'll personally chat with anyone at the station who thinks they can tease you about this. Aiden can be quite convincing."

"Great. Just great." She sighed, sinking into their embrace. "Guess there are worse things I could be. And Ms. December did bring us all together."

"Hell, yeah. Now rest. Because Aiden wants his turn, and after all that sass… You might not see the light of day until December is gone."

About the Author

Author, single mother, slave to chaos—she's a jack-of-all-trades who's constantly looking for her ever elusive clone.

Kris started writing some years back, and it took her a while to realize she wasn't destined for the padded room, and that the voices chattering away in her head were really other characters trying to take shape—and since they weren't telling her to conquer the human race, she went with it. Though she supposes if they had…insert evil laugh.

Kris loves writing erotic novels. She loves heroines who kick butt, heroes who are larger than life and sizzling sex scenes that leave you feeling just a bit breathless.

Kris Norris loves to hear from readers. You can find her contact information, website details and author profile page at http://www.totallybound.com.

Totally Bound Publishing